COLBY NIGHTS

BOOK 2 OF THE COLBY PD SERIES

I0659113

Colby Nights
A Colby PD Book
By Ronnie Ashmore

Published by Creative Texts Publishers, LLC
PO Box 50
Barto, PA 19504
www.creativetexts.com

ISBN: 978-1-64738-054-0

COLBY NIGHTS
BOOK 2 OF THE COLBY PD SERIES

RONNIE ASHMORE

As always, this is for my family.
Thanks for believing in me.

TABLE OF CONTENTS

Chapter 1

Lieutenant Jimmy Williams walked toward the door of the convenience store with his coffee in hand. It was an old-style wooden door that was befitting of the old minute-mart store. As he reached for the knob, the door opened inward with enough force to hit him in the body, causing him to spill his coffee. The hot liquid splashed from his Styrofoam cup and splattered the front of his uniform shirt, burning the hand holding the cup. The young boy who was the cause of the commotion stared wild eyed at the big police officer.

"You always run into stores and people like that, son?" Jimmy asked, trying to wipe the liquid off his navy-blue uniform shirt and hide his annoyance with the boy. It was just after eight in the morning, way too early for this, Jimmy thought.

"No sir, I'm sorry, but you gotta come quick. He's gonna kill 'er," the boy said, running out of the store.

Jimmy followed him outside, throwing the half empty cup in the trash can by the door.

"Go where? Who?"

"The man down there by the bank," the boy said pointing, jumping up and down in place. Jimmy could not see anything from where he was.

He got in his patrol car and followed the kid as he ran down the street toward a crowd of people. He picked up his car radio and called it in.

"Dispatch, I got a possible disturbance in front of the bank on Chestnut. I'll be on scene. Send me backup."

He saw a crowd gathered around looking at something. He could not see the cause of the commotion yet.

Getting out of his car he heard the crowd yelling and shouting. He pushed his way through them and saw a man beating on a female. The woman was in serious trouble.

The man was standing over her as she lay unmoving on the ground. He was holding a handful of her dark hair in one hand while continuously hitting her with his other fist. The impacts made a flat, sick sound as his fist contacted the woman's already beaten, bloody face.

Jimmy tried to stop the man by grabbing him by his arm. The man pulled away turning to face Jimmy, looking him in the eyes.

The man was shorter than Jimmy and not as big, but his eyes appeared to be looking straight through Jimmy to some other object only he could see. His long dark hair was sweat-soaked and dripping droplets onto the sidewalk.

His knuckles of his right hand were mangled and cut. Blood, a mixture of his and hers, rolled off the end of his fingers mixing with the sweat droplets on the pavement.

"You're under arrest. Put your hands behind your back," Jimmy said, reaching for the man again.

"I ain't goin'," he said taking a swing at Jimmy.

Jimmy blocked the blow and swung a right hand at the man's face. The man took the brunt of the punch on the jaw, but never slowed down. He charged at Jimmy full force knocking him off balance. The man fell to the ground. Jimmy staggered backwards but remained standing.

Jimmy reached for the man again while he was on the ground. He rolled away jumping to his feet and came up holding a knife he pulled from a hip pocket of his jeans.

The man activated the spring-loaded knife, opening a blade of about six inches. Jimmy backed away a few steps giving commands as he removed his service pistol from his holster getting the man in his sights.

"Put the knife down. Get on the ground."

Jimmy was yelling full voice as panic and adrenaline surged through his body.

A knife is a serious threat at any distance, but in a close quarter fight, a knife attack could be devastating. The man laughed at Jimmy as he closed the distance.

"Don't make me hurt you," Jimmy said.

The stranger continued walking toward Jimmy, slicing the knife in the air in front of him back and forth. Laughing louder, he lunged at Jimmy.

Jimmy shot him twice, low in the abdomen. The Glock 22 recoiled in his hand. The gunshots were loud as they echoed off the downtown buildings. The man kept walking toward Jimmy, laughing, seemingly unaware he had been shot twice. Jimmy shot him two more times, both shots center mass in the chest. This time the man fell on the sidewalk. He groaned once, then stopped moving.

Jimmy stepped toward the man kicking the knife out of his reach. He placed his fingers of his left hand on the man's neck checking for a sign of life. He found no pulse. He holstered his Glock and went to check the female victim.

He could feel a weak pulse. Her face was beaten severely, both eyes were swollen shut, and cuts from numerous wounds were bleeding profusely. She was unconscious and appeared to be dead. He keyed the lapel mic of his portable radio.

"Dispatch, shots fired. Suspect down. Need EMS and a supervisor to this location now. Where's my backup?" he said talking fast and breathing heavily.

"Ten-four." the dispatcher responded.

Sirens filled the air as the backup unit finally arrived. Jimmy looked around at the crowd. They had moved back several feet and were staring at him. The second officer walked up to Jimmy.

"You okay?" Amy Roberts asked.

"Yeah. Better than him," Jimmy said motioning towards the man. As he pointed, he saw his hand was shaking. He put his hand down by his side.

Amy Roberts was the only female police officer in Colby. She usually worked evenings, so Jimmy was confused as to why she was here.

"Why you?" he asked not able to form his complete thought.

"Chief called me in. I was on my way to the station."

"Chief? I need to call him."

"Did you not hear your radio? Dispatch just told him. He's coming."

Jimmy looked at her and nodded, then looked at the crowd. He looked back at the beaten, bloodied

5

female. He sat down on the sidewalk and waited. He knew the chaos that would soon ensue.

Chapter 2

Amy Roberts left Jimmy sitting on the sidewalk as Chief B. J. Tolliver came walking up. She went to talk to the witnesses from the crowd. She was going to be busy separating people and taking statements from the two dozen or so witnesses.

A pair of EMS paramedics rushed to the man and woman. The one checking the man looked at Tolliver and shook his head. Tolliver watched silently as the other EMS personnel worked over the female. The first one came back, draping a white sheet over the dead man. Tolliver walked over to Jimmy who was sitting in his car.

"You okay?" Tolliver asked.

"Yeah. I guess," Jimmy said, getting out and standing with the Chief.

"Who are they?"

"I don't know either one of them. She's beat so bad her momma wouldn't recognize her."

"Well, captain is on his way. I already had dispatch call the Rangers. You be quiet now. Don't say nothing until it's time," Tolliver said.

Jimmy nodded. B.J. Tolliver had been Chief of Police for over twenty-five years in Colby. He had been with the department for forty-six.

In small departments the Texas Rangers investigated officer-involved shootings. The last one was a year ago. The rangers were efficient and good at their job as a whole.

Tolliver's thoughts were interrupted as he saw the Justice of the Peace approach the dead man. In Texas, a justice of the peace, in his role as coroner, had to be the one to declare a person dead on scene. Only then would it be official.

Chief Tolliver walked up to the JP who stood over the dead man looking down at him. The ambulance had already left for the hospital with the female.

"You know him, Chief?" Judge Bob Harkins asked.

"No."

"I ain't standing here all day. He's dead. When the Ranger gets here and y'all get his identifiers, call me," Harkins said. He was approaching eighty years old and had no patience for the intricacies of his job anymore.

Tolliver nodded glancing back at his lieutenant. Jimmy had never shot anyone before today. Tolliver noticed he just kept staring off not looking at anything. Tolliver walked back to him.

"Jimmy, I want you to go back to the office and wait there."

"Yes sir."

"Collins is on his way. When he gets here, ride with him to the station."

Mike Collins was the last officer to shoot someone. He shot two people in the same family in the same week. They leaned on the hood of Jimmy's car watching Amy come toward them with a handful of papers.

"Chief, I got statements and identifiers for the Ranger," Amy said. She looked at Jimmy, "You okay, Lieutenant?"

He nodded, saying nothing.

"Collins is here. Jimmy, you go on."

Tolliver waited until Jimmy walked off then looked at Roberts. "Find out where the ranger is. And set up a perimeter to keep these people back."

Amy hurried off. Tolliver watched as a new pickup pulled up to the area. A man got out and Tolliver grimaced. Texas Ranger Bart Murphy came walking toward Tolliver. Murphy was a rude, arrogant man that Tolliver did not like much, though they remained professional toward each other on the job.

"Chief, what do you know?" Murphy asked not wasting time with small talk.

His voice was gravelly, the smell of cigarettes wafted from the clothes he was wearing.

"My Lieutenant is the officer involved. JP has pronounced and ambulance took the female half of this to the hospital. The particulars will be at the office for you. We got preliminary statements and identifiers for the witnesses."

"Where is your lieutenant?" Murphy asked, looking around.

"Office."

"Let me look at my body. Crime scene will be here in a bit to collect evidence. Autopsy at Lubbock," he said, walking toward the dead man.

Tolliver followed along listening. Standing over looking at the corpse, Tolliver spoke to the ranger.

"Like always, the shooting is yours. This man's reason for beating the hell outta that little girl is ours."

"He looks like a doper. Got no interest in local meth heads." Murphy walked away.

Tolliver watched him go. He looked around and saw Captain Jim Morgan talking to Amy. He motioned for them to come to him.

"Jim, stay close to Murphy. I wanna know what he finds out." Tolliver looked at Amy, "Follow me back to the office."

Chapter 3

Jimmy was quiet on the ride to the station. Mike Collins could not get any response to his questions, so he decided to stay quiet.

Mike knew a little bit of what his lieutenant was feeling. Last year had been rough on him when he had his shooting. Murphy had not helped much in the beginning.

Mike pulled into the parking lot of the station. They made their way inside the office. Jimmy walked silently to his office leaving Mike alone in the hallway. He went to the patrol room and sat down at a computer to surf the web while he waited. A moment later Jimmy came in and sat down heavily.

"Tell me. What happens now?"

"The ranger, probably Murphy, is already there. Crime scene will collect their evidence. You will be placed on leave and the case will be worked out," Mike said, looking at Jimmy.

"I never shot anyone before."

"I hadn't either, until I did. If the shoot was good, you got nothing to worry over."

They heard the door chime go off indicating someone entered the lobby from outside. The hallway door opened. Tolliver came in and saw them in the patrol room. He motioned for them to follow him to his office. Mike stood in the doorway and Jimmy stood in front of the chief's desk as Tolliver sat down.

"You need to give me your weapon and body camera."

Jimmy unholstered his pistol and placed it on the desk. "I don't have a body camera."

Tolliver looked at him but said nothing. Jimmy continued.

"I didn't turn it on. I forgot to activate it. Car camera was on though," Jimmy said, referring to the dash camera mounted in the patrol cars. The camera would activate if the lights were turned on.

"Did you turn your lights on? They weren't on when I got there." Tolliver asked.

He started to speak. Tolliver raised a hand stopping him.

"No. Don't say anything. Murphy will be here in a while. I do suggest you take some time before talking to him. Understand?"

"Yes sir."

"I have to place you on leave until this investigation is over. Maybe a modified duty assignment."

"I know."

Tolliver motioned for him to leave the office. Jimmy walked out as Tolliver looked at Collins.

"Go to the hospital. Find out who that girl is."

Mike had no idea what girl the chief was talking about. He didn't even know a girl was involved. The chief did not look like he was in the mood for questions though, so Mike decided he would figure it out on his own. He left not asking anything.

At the hospital Mike went straight to the ER trauma area. There he stood around trying not to be in the way of the nurses and aides rushing in and out of rooms. The emergency room was busy this morning with a waiting room full of people needing to be seen. A nurse stopped in front of him and stared, her blond hair draping her shoulders where it had fell from the bun on her head.

"You need something?" she asked.

"I need information on the woman brought in earlier."

The nurse raised her eyebrows and looked around at the busy rooms. "What female?"

Mike was feeling he should have asked more questions of the chief. Tolliver always gave just enough information that you thought you knew what he wanted.

"I don't know. Came from downtown about two hours ago. I don't know her name."

"Oh, her. She's in for X-rays and scans now. I will get you her name."

The nurse copied the information from the file.

"Name is Brenda Perkins. Here is the rest of it," she said, handing him a piece of paper.

Folding the piece of paper, he placed it in his shirt pocket. He thanked her and left the busy emergency room. As he came back into the waiting room, Amy Roberts stood waiting for him.

"Amy, what are you doing?"

"Chief wants us to go to whoever this girl is house and see who is there. Morgan is working on a warrant for the man's house now. Man is Tolbert Ridney from Petersburg."

"The girl is Brenda Perkins, twenty-two years old. Address on Cottonwood. She's still being examined," Mike said.

They decided to take two cars to the Cottonwood address in case of problems. Mike led the way to the address. The house was at one time a nice single-story brick house, but now it was in disrepair, in need a roof and paint. They both looked for any dangers as they approached the front door.

There was no doorbell. Mike knocked loudly. He heard movement inside. He knocked again, and the door came open mid-knock. An elderly lady in a wheelchair opened the door. She looked up at them strangely.

"I only move so fast, you know?" She said, her smoker's voice thick with annoyance.

"Begging your pardon, ma'am. I am looking for the home of Brenda Perkins."

"My granddaughter? Why?" She said, rolling her chair back and inviting them in. Collins stayed on the porch not going in.

"She's been hurt. She's at the E.R. now."

"How?" her voice becoming weak. Tears welled in her eyes, "Was it that damn boy, Tolly?" She asked.

"What can you tell us about him?" Amy asked.

"I know he's a damn dope head. I know that." She was crying in full now.

"Is this man married to your granddaughter?"

"God no. Though he got her hooked on that dope. I need to call my sister to take me to the hospital."

"Yes Ma'am. We will have someone come talk to you in a little while."

The door closed as Mike realized he had forgot to ask her name.

Chapter 4

Jimmy Williams left the police station as Collins was leaving for the hospital. For a moment he thought of going along. He did not like feeling helpless like this. He abandoned the thought. Chief was already a little upset, he would explode if Jimmy defied orders to go home.

There was nothing to go home to though. He lived alone in a small house that he had lived in since returning from college at Texas Tech University. He was a star quarterback here in Colby and at Tech, but a hit from a linebacker who was NFL material ended his career. The hit separated his throwing shoulder and losing the scholarship separated his academics. Instead, he went to the police academy and was hired by Chief Tolliver.

Jimmy was thinking of all that on the drive to his house. He entered the front door and placed his keys in the bowl on the table in the entry. As he made his way to his bedroom, he reached for the pistol that was always in the holster. He remembered it was not there. Removing his duty belt, he hung it inside the closet door in his bedroom. He sat down heavily on bed.

Jimmy thought of calling his parents. They would hear the news soon if they had not already. Small towns were rumor mills where news, whether true or not, spread like wildfire.

His mom and dad still lived outside Colby. His dad was the County Commissioner for the precinct he lived in.

He knew he should call, he just couldn't. Not yet.

He replayed the events of the morning. The man had been wild with rage, continuously beating on a person, a girl, until she was unconscious, then beating on her more. That seemed insane. What kind of drugs was the man on that he could take four 9mm bullets in the torso before falling dead? He shook his head to clear those thoughts. He would have to talk to the ranger soon enough.

He remembered how Murphy had questioned Mike Collins last year during his shooting. He was not looking forward to talking to the ranger. He wanted to know the names of the people involved. He felt he needed to know.

He got his cellphone and called Collins. After three rings he answered.

"Hello?"

"Mike, it's me. You know who the two were from this morning?"

There was silence as Collins hesitated in giving the information.

"Come on. I'm on leave for now. I just want to know."

"She is Brenda Perkins from here. He is Tolbert Ridney from Petersburg. That's all I'm comfortable telling you now, Lieutenant."

Collins hung up. Jimmy tossed the phone on the bed, stood, and cursed. He didn't recognize the names. He changed out of his uniform into his jeans and snap shirt.

He needed to do something. He was not going to sit at home and mope around the house. He would go…The ringing phone interrupted his thoughts. He checked the caller ID. It was his mom.

Chapter 5

B.J. Tolliver sat at his desk after Jimmy and Mike left thinking of the morning and the last few years in general. Three officer involved shootings in less than five years: an officer, a sergeant, who was no longer on the force was first, then Collins last year, now Jimmy. Prior to Sergeant Marten's incident, Tolliver could not remember the last shooting.

He felt tired and worn out. He was going to be sixty-five in a few months. There was no mandatory retirement in Colby, but he considered sixty-five to be about the right age to retire. Truth was he had been considering it for a couple of years now. He had been with the Colby Police Department since he was eighteen years old starting as a dispatcher. But now this job seemed to be all he had in his life.

His wife had died a few years back. They had plans to travel when he did retire. She always told him he was taking his sweet time in retiring. Then she had an aneurism and died suddenly. Now, he was unsure if he wanted to retire or stay until they carried him out from behind this desk. A knock on the door broke his thoughts. He looked up. It was Mike Collins.

"Chief, I got a name for the girl. I talked to the grandmother, but I didn't get her name. She was upset as you can imagine."

"Fine. Do you know if Morgan is back yet?"

"No sir. He ain't."

Tolliver stood, getting his pistol from his desk drawer, and said, "Let's go back to the scene."

Tolliver followed Mike outside to the parking lot. They got in the chief's car as Mike drove them back downtown to the scene. Tolliver saw that everything was almost normal. The man's body was gone, on its way for autopsy no doubt, and the crime scene van Ranger Murphy called in from DPS was gone, too. Murphy's pickup was still parked in the middle of the street and some Colby PD uniform officers still had the street blocked. Captain Jim Morgan was standing next to Murphy talking as Mike and Tolliver approached.

"Well?"

"Chief, you know not a single person called 911 to report this. What kind of world is it where people stand around and watch a girl get the hell beat out of her and don't call the police?" Murphy said, writing in his notebook. He finished and looked around.

"We are done here. I'll need to talk to Williams."

"Tomorrow. I sent him home earlier. His gun is at the office."

Murphy nodded saying nothing.

"Jim, when you're done here, we got the girl identified."

Morgan nodded. Ranger Murphy would investigate the shooting, but the rest of the investigation was a Colby PD investigation. Tolliver wanted to make sure they found out everything.

Tolliver walked back to his car with Mike.

"Have Roberts come get you. Y'all go patrol or something."

Tolliver got in his car and drove away, leaving Mike standing in the street.

Chapter 6

Mike was waiting on the sidewalk when Amy pulled up to get him. He got in and she started driving, not saying a word. Mike broke the silence.

"He just left me there." He shook his head.

"You know the chief. He can be cantankerous," Amy said, trying to calm him down.

"I don't know what's wrong with him."

Amy decided to try and calm Mike down another way.

"You want to go somewhere for dinner tonight?" She asked.

"I don't know. We always go out of town. Why can't we get dinner here in town?"

"You know why."

Mike and Amy had been dating the last six months. Amy was a couple of years younger than Mike, but she did not seem to mind that. There was no rule about dating co-workers, but they both felt it was better not to advertise the relationship in town too much. Sometimes the frustration was more than either would admit to the other. Despite that, they managed to go out like normal people and even stay at each other's house a couple of times a week.

"Let's go to the hospital and see if that Perkins girl can talk to us," Mike said.

"Chief told us to patrol."

"He said patrol or something. I'd rather do something."

Amy agreed and headed toward the hospital.

At the hospital they went to the check in desk to ask about Perkins. She was in ICU and not allowed visitors. They saw her grandmother in her wheelchair coming around the corner heading their way. Amy took the lead in speaking with her.

"Ma'am, remember us? We would like to talk to you some more."

She continued to wheel outside through the automatic doors.

"About what?" She said, stopping to light a cigarette.

"I understand she is in ICU," Amy said.

"Yeah. Broken eye socket, jaw broke in two places, fractured skull, broken ribs, and a collapsed lung. Real swell guy that Tolly is." She wiped a tear from her eye and took a puff of her cigarette.

"How bad is Brenda's drug habit?" Mike asked.

"Bad enough. She was a great kid. Smart. That guy turned her into an addict. Where is he?"

"Dead, ma'am," Roberts said. The grandmother smiled as she exhaled smoke.

"What is your name?" Mike asked, taking his note pad from his uniform shirt pocket.

"Elinore Perkins."

Mike wrote her information down as she gave it to him. She told them she was trying to take care of her granddaughter that was just out of jail for writing hot checks. Brenda had moved in with her about six months ago and then met Tolly Ridney at a bar or something. Ridney was bad news. She tried to warn Brenda, but she wouldn't listen. She crushed her cigarette out in the ashtray.

She looked at the two cops and said, "I need to fix my baby, now. Excuse me." She wheeled back inside the hospital.

Chapter 7

Jimmy Williams sat at his parent's table and told the story again. His mother, Margaret, insisted on hearing it again. She shook her head in the same places and made the same sighs in the same spots during each retelling. Jimmy was tired of telling it. His father, Will, listened silently each time.

"That's it. That's what happened," Jimmy said, sipping his sweet tea from a mason jar his mother used as a drinking glass.

"That's horrible, Jimmy. You need a different line of work. Maybe your dad can get you on with the county," she said, looking at her husband and nodding her head.

"Now, Maggie, the boy is alright. Besides, this is his first major incident."

Will was now the elected county commissioner, though he started as a road crew member. He had been with the county all of Jimmy's life.

"I don't want to work at the county, Mom. I'm doing what I want to do. What Grandpa did before me. I like my job."

His grandfather was chief of police in Colby for years. It was George Williams who hired B.J. Tolliver to be a dispatcher over forty something years ago. Jimmy took pride in his legacy at the police department and was looking forward to being chief himself when Tolliver retired.

"I just worry about you," she said, picking up the empty pie plates from the table, taking them to the kitchen for washing.

"Your mom will be okay," his dad said, watching her go.

"I know."

"You need to take care of yourself. Don't let this get ya down. I got to go back to work."

"I'll follow you out."

They stepped out on the front porch of the old house that Jimmy was raised in. It sat on five acres that seemed so large when he was a kid with no neighbors around. Now it felt like neighbors were encroaching on the edges and pushing their way in. Jimmy still enjoyed being there. His mom usually had a family meal once a month where cousins and all kinds of kinfolk showed up. Jimmy was an only child, so he enjoyed the cousins most of the time.

"I got to go to the office, Dad. I'll see ya later."

Jimmy left the farmhouse and drove the four miles back to town. At the police station he saw that

Morgan's pickup was in the lot. He wanted to talk to Morgan to find out what they knew.

He looked inside Morgan's office. No one there. He heard voices from the Chief's office. He knocked on the frame of the door. Tolliver motioned for him to come in.

"Thought you went home?" Tolliver said.

"At my mom's. She had to see me," Jimmy said, sitting down.

"How is lady Margaret?"

Tolliver had called her that since before Jimmy was born it seemed. His mom loved it and always smiled when addressed like that.

"Good. We know anything yet?"

"Roberts and Collins interviewed the Grandmother," Martin said, looking at his notes in front of him. "She says Tolbert Ridney was a real winner. Brenda Perkins, the girl, did county time for hot checks. Got mixed up with this clown and now is in ICU broken in pieces."

"Bad?"

"Bad enough," Tolliver said, giving him the rundown on the girl's injuries.

"If you hadn't shot him grandma probably would have," Morgan said. Jimmy looked over at him.

"Too soon?" Morgan asked.

"Jimmy, you got to talk to Ranger Murphy tomorrow. After that I'm going to put you on a special task to find out all you can about Tolbert Ridney. I wanna know why he went crazy and beat on her so badly," Tolliver said, standing up.

Knowing they had just been dismissed, Morgan and Jimmy left the chief's office. Morgan stopped at his office. Jimmy went back home.

Chapter 8

Chief Tolliver was at the office before seven the next morning. He enjoyed being at the office before everything got chaotic in the day. He stayed late most nights for the same reason. He turned on his desk light and sat down to sort papers.

Tolbert Ridney was on his mind this morning. Captain Morgan would have a warrant to search his house in Petersburg today. Since Petersburg was in another county, that Sheriff's Office would assist in the search. Tolliver knew Morgan could handle the search alone, but he was going to send Collins with him. He picked up the phone and told dispatch to call Collins in.

He knew of Elinor Perkins, the girl's grandmother. It was hard to do this job this long in the same town and not know a lot of people. In her younger days, Elinor Perkins, Elie as she was called then, was a troublemaker, too. Marijuana was about the worst drug in the area then, but alcohol was always around. Alcohol was Elie's problem. She was a bad drunk back then and mean. The police used to have to fight her every time they dealt with her.

Elinor was in that wheelchair because of alcohol. She was drunk and wrecked her car out in the county one night, years ago. The car was destroyed and so was Elinor Perkins' legs.

The door chime interrupted his thoughts. He glanced at his wall clock, nearly eight-thirty. He had daydreamed about the past for over an hour, Tolliver thought. Mike Collins knocked on the open door.

"Turn on the lights, huh."

Mike flipped the switch lighting up the office.

"You wanted me here?"

Tolliver motioned for him to sit down, then said, "I want you to go with Morgan to Petersburg this morning."

Tolliver cleared his throat not sure how to approach the next subject.

"Listen, you know since Rod Marten left for the game warden job, we have a sergeant slot open. I want you to have it."

"Me? Really? I never thought about that," Mike said.

"Yeah, well, I want you to have it, but you bein' sergeant could be a conflict with your relationship with Amy Roberts."

Mike's smile disappeared, replaced with silent dread. He decided to remain silent.

"You didn't think you could hide that from me, now did you?" Tolliver asked, staring at Mike.

"No, sir. We weren't really trying to hide it much."

"Well, I ain't one to tell a man about his personal business. I need to decide if you can be supervisor over someone you are…, um, involved with. And please, I don't want to know how involved."

Mike stayed silent.

Tolliver motioned for him to leave his office. He smiled as he watched Collins left. These young guys thought they could hide things from the old chief, Tolliver thought.

It was good to let them know he knew more than they thought. Tolliver thought again of Ridney and remembered Jimmy was going to talk to the ranger this morning.

Chapter 9

Jimmy Williams walked into the police station like a man walking to his execution. He had slept poorly last night, and this morning he felt a sense of dread in coming here to talk to the ranger. He tried his best to hide his nervousness. Collins and Morgan passed him in the hallway on their way out the door.

"You'll be fine, Jimmy," Collins said in passing.

Jimmy nodded and smiled. Ranger Murphy was waiting in the conference room for him. He went in and took a seat on the other side of the table from Murphy. Murphy reached back and closed the door, which slammed hard enough to startle Jimmy.

"Damn, sorry about that. Didn't know it would slam," Murphy said, pulling papers from his binder.

He slid a statement form toward Jimmy.

"I'll need a written statement, but first, let's go over what happened. I am recording this, too, so you know." He activated the voice recorder on the table. He gave the introductions of who was in the room as well as date and time.

"You are James Michael Williams. You currently hold the rank of Lieutenant with the Colby Police Department. Correct?"

"Yes sir," Jimmy said, clearing his throat.

"Tell me about the events that occurred on the date in question."

Taking a deep breath, Jimmy told the story again. Twenty minutes later Jimmy was finished. Murphy sat there silent writing in his notebook. When he finished writing he looked up at Jimmy.

"Why no video?" Murphy asked, then started writing again.

"I forgot to turn my body camera on. I thought I had activated my overheads for the dash camera to record."

"I have witness statements from the onlookers. They say, for the most part, you took your time coming to help. Explain that."

"That's wrong. I went down there as soon as the kid told me. I got there as fast as I could," Jimmy said, sitting up in his chair.

"Why did you not use something less lethal? Pepper spray, Taser, whatever?" Murphy asked, still writing not looking up.

"I didn't have time. It escalated too quickly."

"Is it true you were mad at being interrupted in your morning routine and you went down there looking to hurt someone? You didn't mean to kill him, but you were looking to take your anger out on somebody." Murphy looked up and stared at Jimmy.

"That is not true. I did what I had to do. He came at me with the knife. Surely your witnesses told you that." Jimmy sat on the edge of his chair clinching his fists.

"Okay. We're done." Turning off the voice recorder Murphy continued, "Fill out the statement form with your version of events. I'll leave you alone to finish it."

Jimmy stared at the ranger as he walked out the door. Collins was right. Murphy was a dick. Jimmy wrote his statement in forty-five minutes. He did not know if he was to wait on Murphy or go find him. He stood as the door opened.

"Done? Okay. I will be in touch if I need anything."

Chapter 10

Mike and Captain Morgan were making the ninety plus mile drive to Petersburg in mostly silence. Mike was lost in his own thoughts about what Chief Tolliver had said to him earlier about Amy. He had not had a chance to call or text to let her know the chief knew. He wondered if he was even supervisor material. He looked over at Morgan who was focused on his driving.

"Captain, can I ask you something?"

"What?"

"Chief wants me to be sergeant. I want it too, but I had never thought of being a supervisor until Chief mentioned it. What do you think?"

"Sergeant? Yeah, you got the experience and I think you'd make a good supervisor. The troops like you. What about you and Amy, though?" Morgan said, looking in his direction.

Mike was silent and faced back toward the windshield. How did he know? How did anyone know?

"You think you can keep secrets like that in a small town?" Morgan said, laughing.

"I thought we were being careful. Forget I asked." He was sorry he ever mentioned anything.

"What's the address we are looking for?"

Mike located an address from a file sitting in the middle of the seat and read them aloud. Morgan navigated his way to the street. As they turned onto the street, they saw two sheriff patrol cars waiting in front of a house.

The house was wood framed, painted green with blue trim. There was no vehicle in the driveway. Collins read in the report where Ridney's old Camaro had been towed from in front of the bank after the shooting. They parked and got out introducing themselves to the two deputies.

"We have had problems with Tolly for a long time," said the deputy named Richardson.

"Is he in jail?" asked the other one. Ames was etched on the nameplate above his right uniform shirt pocket.

"Dead. One of our guys shot him yesterday," Morgan said, as they walked to the front porch.

"Shame about that. He was a piece of shit. Dealt a lot of dope from this house," Ames said. His tone conveyed nobody from the sheriff's office would miss Tolbert Ridney very much.

Morgan tried the doorknob. It turned freely in his hand. He opened the door easy, looking for dogs or people, either one. The house was empty. The smell of stale booze and cigarettes slapped them in the face.

The house was trashed. As they entered into the living area, Mike saw empty beer cans and bottles lying everywhere. Trash was piled high in various corners of the living room with a horrid stench coming from the kitchen. Mike sagged a little knowing they had to search this dump.

"Well, if he weren't dead, we could've indicted for felony housekeeping," Morgan said, pulling on a pair of rubber gloves.

The two deputies laughed. Mike did not. He made his way to the single bedroom. It was as messy as the main part of the house. On a bedside table was evidence of Tolbert Ridney's habit. A decorative marijuana pipe and a glass pipe used to smoke methamphetamine were lying on the table next to a baggie of marijuana.

"We wanna bag the dope?" Mike yelled.

"Not our dope investigation. Not our jurisdiction," Morgan yelled back.

Two hours later Mike and Morgan had found nothing to let them know why Ridney was in Colby. They left the two deputies to gather the drugs and the paraphernalia. It was a long drive back home.

Chapter 11

Chief Tolliver wanted some lunch. He decided to walk to the diner down the street for his usual meal. The diner was his favorite place to eat in town partly because the food was good but mostly because it was within walking distance.

He met a man coming in the office as he was headed out.

"Going to lunch, Chief?" The man asked, standing in front of the exit door blocking the path.

"Well, Councilman Rice. Yes, care to join me?" Councilman Joe Rice was one of the longest serving members on the current council. He was an ardent supporter of the police department in general and B.J. Tolliver in particular.

"Sure. We walking?"

The men stepped out in the sunshine as Rice put his sunglasses on.

"What brings you over here?" Tolliver asked, knowing this was not a social visit.

Rice sighed as they continued walking, "The council, some members anyway, are concerned."

"About?"

"The shooting yesterday. The young girl getting beat senseless on a main street in town. Your ability to handle the pressures of this job anymore." Rice looked at Tolliver through the dark sunglasses waiting for a reaction.

Tolliver grinned, "I know who's worried about me handling the pressure. Janet Long. That woman has never wanted me in this job."

"She is one voice. But not the only voice."

"You?" Tolliver asked, as they reached the door to the diner.

"Chief, you know I'm your biggest supporter on that board. I'm here telling you so you won't get blindsided on the street."

Tolliver opened the diner door, and they walked in. The cooking smells made Tolliver realize how hungry he was. The diner was empty of patrons as it was early yet. They seated themselves at a table in the back of the diner as the waitress took their drink orders.

"Listen. I ain't worried about Long being mad at me. She thinks her election to the board is a green light to get rid of me. I know this shootin' was tragic for the officer involved. The bad guy made the choice to end it that way."

"Well, Miss Long wants to meet with you and me tomorrow in her office to discuss 'matters' as she put it."

"Fine. I will meet with her only but in my office. I will only tell her what I can and no more. Now let's eat and forget about Janet Long. Thinking of her hurts my appetite."

Rice laughed. They spent the rest of the meal discussing other matters.

Returning to his office after parting ways with Joe Rice, Tolliver sat down heavily in his chair, his mind running wild. Was this the event the council was waiting for to have enough justification to fire him? Why would this event spark this much outrage?

The more he thought about it the angrier he became. He took a deep breath and forced himself to calm down. He picked up his desk phone and pressed the speed dial button for Jimmy Williams. Jimmy answered on the fourth ring.

"Jimmy, I need you here as soon as you can. I got one of those modified assignments for you."

He hung up and sat back in his chair still feeling out of sorts.

Chapter 12

An hour later Jimmy Williams pulled into the parking lot of the police station the same time as Mike and Morgan arrived back from their trip to Petersburg. The three exchanged greetings in the parking lot and walked to the chief's office together.

Tolliver looked up from his desk as they all walked in. Jimmy and Morgan sat in the two chairs in front of the desk while Mike stood in his usual place by the file cabinets in the corner. Morgan gave a rundown on what they found at Ridney's house.

"Sounds like a real upstanding citizen. I called Murphy for a report on the drug screen for him. He will bring that by later this evening."

"Chief, we need to talk to the girl. Maybe she can tell us something," Morgan said.

"I agree. Mike, you and Jimmy go to the hospital. Find out what you can on Ridney and her relationship. Morg, I want you to reach out to your informants. See where he would buy meth here."

"Chief, you sure you want me going?" Jimmy asked.

"You feel up to it?" Tolliver asked, Jimmy nodded, "Good. Now y'all go on."

Since Jimmy was in his personal car and unable to drive the city car, Mike drove his patrol unit to the hospital. Mike was curious about Jimmy's interview with Murphy.

"How did it go this morning?"

"Murphy is not on my Christmas card list."

"Yeah, did he tell you you were looking to kill someone? He used that one on me. Pissed me off," Mike said.

Jimmy said nothing. Mike did not push it. They rode the rest of the way in silence. At the hospital reception desk, they were told Brenda Perkins was in a regular room. The lady gave them the room number, and the two made their way down the hall to the room. The hospital smelled of antiseptic and cleaners which burned the nose.

At the room door Jimmy knocked, opening the door slowly. They walked inside the room. Brenda Perkins was alone and watched them enter. She had a thick bandage wrapped around her head like a bandana. Her face had several bandages in different areas covering stitches, no doubt. She tried talking but the wires in her jaw prevented her from making any more than a hissing sound.

"Miss Perkins. I'm Mike Collins. This is Lieutenant Jimmy Williams. We are with the police department. Can we ask you some questions?"

She mumbled and hissed. She swallowed then pointed to a notepad on the bedside table. Jimmy handed it and the pen to her. She started writing.

She held up the note pad. In big letters she had written yes.

"Was Tolbert Ridney your boyfriend?" Jimmy asked.

She wrote again, yes. Was?

"He was killed attacking the officer who tried to stop him beatin' on you," Mike said.

She nodded. Then started writing again.

As she was writing Mike asked, "You know where he got his drugs from?"

She was writing faster now. She held up the notepad for them to see. 'We were supposed to break up. Went to bank to withdraw money to split. He was high when he picked me up. He got mad because wasn't enough money. He beat the shit out of me. I don't know where he bought from. Who shot him?'

Mike read the questions aloud then looked at Jimmy.

"I did ma'am. It was me who shot him."

Brenda Perkins wrote again. 'Thank you.' She started crying silently. They decided to leave her alone.

Chapter 13

Tolliver turned off the lights in his office, ready to leave for the day. It was early for him to leave, just after five in the evening. He was still a little upset about the news Joe Rice had delivered earlier about the city council. He closed his door trying to forget about it.

He heard the dispatch voice over the scanner in the patrol room. There was a disturbance at a residence on the south side of the city. That area of the city, called poverty point by most locals, was known for its rougher element. People were poor and often out of work. Most of the inhabitants turned to drinking or drugs for their escape.

He listened for officers to respond to dispatch. There should be two on evenings now. Roberts responded that she was going. A patrol officer named Franks, who mainly worked interdiction, told dispatch he would be the back-up unit. Tolliver continued walking out to his patrol car.

As he started the car, his cellphone rang. The dispatcher told him of the call he had just sent Roberts and Franks on. Tolliver told him he would go to the call as well.

While driving to the address, he heard Roberts and Franks check on scene. Tolliver was driving the speed limit with no emergency lights activated.

A few minutes later, Roberts' voice came over the radio in a high pitch yell for backup and asking for other units. She was hard to understand as adrenaline and fear surged through her body. Tolliver's heart rate increased as he listened. He accelerated the patrol unit and activated the emergency lights.

Tolliver pulled up to a house that should have been torn down. The roof was in shambles with loose shingles lying on the ground. There were wooden boards from the front of the house missing. The west Texas sandstorms had removed all paint from the wooden structure long ago.

Roberts was fighting hand to hand with a man in the front yard. He was grabbing at her duty belt, and she was trying to wrestle away from him. Franks had a tight grip on the white undershirt the man had on. Tolliver saw the wire leads hanging from the man's body where either Roberts or Franks had used the less lethal electronic control weapon on the man. The weapon lay forgotten on the ground.

The man threw Roberts to the ground and spun on Franks. He picked Franks up by the duty belt and neck and held him over his head. Tolliver was already rushing to help his officers. The crazy man body slammed Franks to the ground with force. The air rushed from Franks' lungs as he instantly grabbed his back in pain.

Roberts gained her feet as her and Tolliver charged the man, knocking him off balance enough to get him on the ground on his belly. Tolliver straddled his back pinning his arms to his side and at the same time grabbed under the man's chin, pulling his head back with force. The man was making growling sounds and yelling as loud as he could through Tolliver's hold.

Roberts managed to cuff the man's hands. Once the handcuffs were on, the man lost his will to fight. He went limp instantly. Tolliver relaxed his grip and the man started foaming at the mouth. He vomited and coughed white phlegm all over the ground.

Roberts called for an ambulance on her portable radio. Tolliver got off the man and stood. EMS arrived on the scene several minutes later, though it seemed like hours.

As they were unloading their medical equipment, Collins and Williams slid to a stop in the front yard. Tolliver looked over to Franks. He was standing, walking slowly around, trying to shake off the pain.

The handcuffed man was being put on a stretcher. Tolliver asked for Roberts' handheld radio

"Dispatch, call one of the midnight officers. Tell them to meet the ambulance with our prisoner at the hospital." He waited for the reply then handed it back.

"Amy, you okay?" He asked.

Her duty belt was twisted around to where the holster was in front of her uniform pants, her shirt was ripped showing her ballistic vest and the under shirt beneath, and her baton and other equipment were scattered in the yard. She nodded as she gathered her gear.

"Let's find out what we have here," Tolliver said, as they all moved toward the opened front door.

Chapter 14

Mike and Jimmy were heading to the station after leaving the hospital when they heard Roberts' call for backup go out. They arrived on scene in less than seven minutes, but it seemed like hours.

When Jimmy skidded to a stop, they saw Chief Tolliver standing up as Roberts was straightening her uniform. Franks was walking around slowly. Roberts and Franks looked as if they had been fighting with the man for a while. Jimmy approached Franks to find out if he was okay.

Mike fought the urge to run to Amy and check her for injuries. He kept telling himself she was okay. She was walking around and talking, she was okay. Tolliver used her radio then led the way toward the house.

"I'm sending Franks to the hospital to get checked out. Another ambulance is coming," Jimmy said, catching up to the rest of them outside the front door.

"Fine," Tolliver said, as he entered the house first.

The living room was the first room you entered; it was in shambles. Broken furniture was scattered around the room. A coffee table was broken in pieces lying in the center of the floor. Shattered glass from the broken picture frames lay in the stained carpet. The couch had been overturned against the far wall.

As they moved to the kitchen area, the same destruction lay in there too. The refrigerator lay on its side in the floor, with the contents creating a mess on the linoleum floor. A woman sat in the corner of the kitchen between the cookstove and cabinet hugging her knees and shaking.

"Are you okay?" Tolliver asked, picking his way through the mess to stand in front of the crying woman.

She looked at the cops then stood uneasily. Tolliver offered his hand which she took, gaining her feet.

"He went crazy. I came home to cook supper." She cried again, sniffling. "I told him it would be late. He went to the shop out back then came in and started pushing me and throwing things. He said awful things to me. He just went crazy."

Jimmy tapped Mike on the shoulder, and they went out the back door to the shop building. As they entered the shop through the open screen door, Mike saw on the floor of the shop a glass pipe that had some methamphetamine residue in it. He picked it up.

Jimmy was looking on the workbenches where tools and car parts were scattered about.

"Look here. His happy bag," Jimmy said, holding up a purple, cloth whiskey bag that many drug users use to keep their materials in.

"I got his pipe," Mike said, walking over to where Jimmy was.

Jimmy opened the bag. Inside was the standard drug user's items. A small baggie of marijuana, a few syringes, and rolling papers for making joints. At the bottom was a clear plastic baggie that contained a crystal substance they both recognized as methamphetamine. Jimmy held it up.

"That meth is darker than what I normally see around here," Mike said, squinting at the baggie.

"Yeah. Wonder why? Let's bag everything, let the lab sort it out."

Mike walked back around front to get evidence bags and a camera from one of the units. Tolliver caught up to him as he was looking for the items.

"Mike, take Amy home. Me and Jimmy will finish here. The victim is writing a statement now. Around midnight you relieve whoever is watching our guy at the hospital."

"Yes sir. I can do that," Mike said, watching as Amy slowly walked to her patrol car and got in on the passenger side.

Chapter 15

Mike left the scene and headed to Amy's house. She was quiet and did not answer when Mike asked if she was hungry. He pulled into a Sonic stall and pushed the red button.

"Get me a number one," Amy said.

Mike ordered their food then turned to look at Amy. She looked disheveled and tired.

"I'm glad you're okay."

"I'm embarrassed. An old man had to help me subdue my prisoner," Amy said, shaking her head, then continuing, "That man was insanely strong for a short, skinny guy. I have never seen anything like it. Scared me, bad. Chief probably saved my life."

"We found his dope in the shop. What's his name?"

"I don't remember."

Mike stared straight ahead thinking. Now was not a good time, but it may be the only time. He had to tell her. He looked back at her.

"Timing sucks, but I need to tell you something. Chief offered me the sergeant slot."

Amy turned, facing him, and smiled, "That's great. I'm happy for you. You'll be a great sergeant."

"There's a catch. He wants to know if being a supervisor will be a conflict with our relationship."

"He knows?" Amy asked, raising her eyebrows.

"Yeah. And guess what? Seems Captain Morgan knows, too."

"How? We have been careful. I thought. Are we in trouble?"

"No. Chief didn't sound mad, just concerned. I won't take the slot if it means giving up what we are building here." He looked at her fully then said, "I'm in love with you, Amy. I will stay on patrol if I have to choose."

Amy looked down at her lap then looked at Mike.

"I'm in love with you, too. But if Chief don't mind, maybe you can have both."

The food arrived. Mike paid the teenage carhop telling her to keep the change. He left the parking lot heading toward Amy's house. He drove, feeling better for telling her how much he loved her and her telling him in response. It would not matter if he got the promotion or not if he had her. He could not hide the smile.

"What's funny?" Amy asked, stealing a fry from the bag.

"Thinking of how you and I came to be. Six months. Best time of my life. Now that we don't have to hide, it can only get better."

Mike saw Amy nod in approval. The case that brought them together was a year ago. It was a hard case to work on, but it ended up being good for them anyway. It took him a couple of months to find the nerve to ask her out, but it had been worth it. He asked one night in the patrol room at shift change. She said yes.

Mike parked in the driveway of her small house on Peach Street. He carried the food in the house while she carried the drink cups and straws. Mike divided the food in the kitchen while Amy changed clothes. She came back wearing shorts and a Texas Tech T-shirt. She touched his arm and turned him toward her. She kissed him lightly on the lips wrapping her arms around him and squeezing firmly. He returned the hug stroking her back gently.

"He scared me, Mike. I need to take a self-defense course. What I learned in the academy didn't work," she said, stepping back. She added ketchup to her fries.

"Whatever you think you need to do." he said.

"I hope I never run into a monster like that again. If the guy the lieutenant shot was acting like that, I can understand him shooting him." She picked up her food and walked toward the living room.

Mike watched her walk away.

Chapter 16

Tolliver walked into the office early like normal. This morning he was to meet with Janet Long of the city council to discuss whatever she wanted to talk about. He had told her he could meet before eight. Hopefully, it would not take long.

Amy Roberts poked her head around the corner.

"Well, you look rested. How are you?" Tolliver asked, motioning for her to sit down.

"Fine. I slept well," she said, sitting in the chair.

"Mike at the hospital still?"

"Sleeping at home, I guess. They released that man to jail early this morning," Amy said.

Tolliver could see she was uncomfortable talking about Mike. He decided to not press that issue. Instead, he looked at a file on his desk and said, "The man is Bobby Springer. He is a welder by trade."

"Thanks for helping me with him. I think I would have been in trouble. What do you want me to do?"

"No problem. I am getting a little old to wrestle on the ground with people, though. This morning, I want you to act like a piece of furniture in this meeting I am going to have in a bit."

The secretary, Joyce, came in and announced that Councilwoman Long was coming into the building. She said she would show her in.

Janet Long entered and noticed the female officer standing in the corner by the file cabinets. Long sat down putting her leather case in the empty chair beside her.

"I thought we were to meet alone, Chief," Long said, looking over her shoulder at Roberts.

"Well, I think it would be good to have a witness in here since we don't really trust each other. Think of her as furniture like a lamp or another file cabinet," Tolliver said, remaining in his chair.

"Very well. What I want to talk about is the future. Since you are more of the past than the future of this department, I want to start thinking of your replacement."

"My replacement has been decided. Lieutenant Williams will make a fine chief of police, like his grandfather before him."

"There's the outdated thinking I'm talking about. I personally don't think Williams is chief material. Him killing that man in cold blood is just one reason I think he is not qualified…"

Tolliver interrupted, "Cold blood? Miss Long you have no idea what you're talkin' about. When you say stuff like that you sound silly. Just silly."

"I may sound silly to you because I'm a woman telling an old dinosaur how I feel."

"No. You sound silly in general, to anyone with common sense. Right, Officer Roberts?"

"Yes sir." Amy answered without hesitating.

"Be that as it may. You have been in this office for a quarter of a century. That is long enough. I will see you out of office before my term is up."

"Listen, I have been here a long time. Forty-six years to be exact with this department. I think I have earned the right to leave on my terms. But I know I have earned the right not to be pushed out of this office by the likes of you. Now, if you'll excuse me, I have work to do," Tolliver said.

Janet Long picked up her leather case and stood. She left the room in a hurry not saying anything.

Tolliver looked at Roberts and said, "I didn't mean to drag you into this. I apologize."

"Don't worry about it Chief. I got your back," Amy said, walking out the door.

Chapter 17

Jimmy Williams sat at his desk. He felt adrift like a boat that slipped its anchor and was just going where the wind blew it. He was on administrative leave, but he was working the case. Not the shooting, of course, but the reason Ridney had committed his act against the Perkins girl. He was nowhere on figuring that out.

Brenda Perkins could not help much when he and Collins interviewed her yesterday at the hospital. Now, he had dope to package for the crime lab from yesterday evening. He needed a vacation he thought. He walked to Captain Morgan's office to get him to release the drugs they recovered from Springer's shop.

"You talk to chief yet?" Morgan asked, handing Jimmy a form to sign.

"Just got here." He returned the form.

"Not a good morning so far. Councilwoman Long was here. Roberts said it got pretty heated. Long wants chief gone," Morgan said, watching Jimmy for a reaction.

"I'll go see him while you get the evidence."

Jimmy knocked on Tolliver's door and waited for Tolliver to look at him.

"Come in. Close the door."

"Morgan said it was a bad morning," Jimmy said, sitting in a chair.

"That woman wants me gone yesterday. She wants to name my replacement."

"Replacement? She knows that has been established," Jimmy said.

"Well, she don't want you in this chair, I'll tell ya that. According to her, you're a cold-blooded killer like we have never seen before."

"What?"

Tolliver waved a dismissive hand in the air, "She's only one voice, but depending on what Murphy finds in the shooting, she may be the loudest," Tolliver said, leaning back in his chair.

"Sounds like it's time to circle the wagons, don't it?"

A knock on the door interrupted the conversation. Jimmy reached back opening the door.

Ranger Bart Murphy and a stranger stood in the doorway. They came in uninvited. Murphy sat next to Jimmy while the stranger remained standing. The stranger was no Texas Ranger You could tell by the clothes he wore as well as the long goatee beard he had. Rangers did not allow that.

"I bring some news from the lab," Murphy said, opening the file. He removed a sheet of paper handing it to Tolliver. "This is Robert Weeps. DPS narcotic investigator. Chief Tolliver and Lieutenant Jimmy Williams."

They all shook hands. Instead of calling the state police by that name, like most states, Texas called their version the Department of Public Safety. They oversaw everything from driver license to the Texas Rangers. It was their lab Colby PD submitted evidence to for testing.

"What is this?" Tolliver asked after scanning over the document.

"Chief, that is the reason your Lieutenant here had to kill Mr. Ridney," Weeps said.

"How's that?" Jimmy asked, looking over his shoulder at him.

"He was high on enough shit to walk from here to Canada. The official name of this particular shit is alpha-pyrrolidinopentiophenone, Alpha-PVP. It's known in some areas as flakka or gravel. It's a synthetic drug also known as bath salts," Weeps said.

Jimmy stood to get a better look at this newcomer with all this knowledge.

"Makes people feel a sense of euphoria and strength. Dopers mix it with meth and cocaine to get a greater high. People on salts by themselves are known to go ape shit crazy, mix it with meth or something else. Look out," Weeps said.

"We had an incident yesterday with a man who was stronger than he should have been. I got some meth I was going to send to the lab. Can you check if this has any of that salt stuff in it?" Jimmy asked.

Weeps said he would take it to Lubbock for testing. In a few minutes Jimmy was back with the drugs that Morgan packaged. He handed the package to Weeps and had him sign the evidence sheet. Jimmy was sure they had their first solid lead to their investigation.

Chapter 18

Mike Collins came to work the evening shift for Officer Franks who had hurt his back wrestling with Bobby Springer yesterday. Evening shift meant he would work for the first time in a long time with Amy Roberts. He was looking forward to the evening shift.

As soon as he entered the patrol room the intercom sounded informing him Chief Tolliver wanted to see him. He walked to the chief's office feeling sure he was not going to like what the assignment would be.

"You want to see me?" Mike asked, stepping into the office.

"I want you to go to the hospital and talk to that Perkins girl again. We need more information on where Ridney got his drugs or who he hung around with."

"Okay." Mike walked away upset that he was having to go question the girl again. He thought they already had all she had to tell.

He drove to the hospital hoping Brenda Perkins would be able to communicate a little better with him today than last time. As he entered her hospital room her grandmother was asleep in her wheelchair. Brenda was watching TV. She looked at Mike as he walked in.

"Hi, I don't want to interrupt. I need to talk to you again. If you can," Mike said, speaking softly not wanting to wake up her grandmother.

"It's fine," Brenda said, she spoke through clenched jaws making her hard to understand, the words running together.

Elinor Perkins woke up and saw Mike standing there.

"Goodness. I didn't know you were there," Elinor said, shifting in the chair.

"Yes, ma'am," Mike said, then turned his attention back to Brenda. "Where did Tolbert Ridney get his drugs from?"

"I told you I don't know," Brenda said.

"I know that's what you said, I just don't fully believe you. Who did he hang around here in Colby?"

"Nobody really," Brenda said, inhaling deeply to suck saliva from her lips as it ran out her mouth.

"Brenda, your boyfriend tried to kill you and a police officer. We need to find out who else is involved in his drug world. We need your help."

"He hung with a guy named…" her voice slurred so much Mike could not understand the name. She tried again, and it slurred again.

Mike handed her a pen and the notebook sitting on the bedside table. She started writing. She wrote for several minutes then handed the pad to Mike. He read it slowly.

'Tolly hung out with a group of guys at the horseshoe bar. They were all into the drinking and drugs. Tolly sold for them sometimes. Usually marijuana. He usually bought from a house down in poverty point. Sheehan was the name on the mailbox I think.'

Mike tore the page off and put it in his pocket. Brenda reached for the tablet again, and Mike handed it to her. She began writing again. When she finished, she handed it back to him.

'Do you know anyone I can talk to who will understand the mess I have made in my life? Not a preacher. I don't want to live like this anymore.'

"Yeah. I know someone. I'll see if I can't get 'em to stop by and visit with you," he said.

She nodded in agreement and Mike took his leave from the room.

Walking to the parking lot he looked again at the paper she had written on. The Horseshoe was a rough bar outside the city in the county jurisdiction. It catered to the rougher elements of the area. He looked at the name she had written down. He did not know anyone named Sheehan.

Chapter 19

Jimmy Williams sat alone in his office with the door closed. He knew Weeps was heading to Lubbock to test the methamphetamine found in Bobby Springer's workshop. Maybe there was a connection between the drugs ingested by Tolbert Ridney and the drugs found in the Springer shop.

His desk phone rang interrupting his thoughts. He answered the phone and listened to the other party, wrote his notes on his calendar, then hung up.

He walked to the chief's office and entered the open door without knocking.

"I gotta go see a doctor?" Jimmy asked, still standing in front of the chief's desk.

"Yeah," Tolliver said, looking up at Jimmy.

"I ain't going. I don't need no doctor telling me what I should be feeling."

"You can feel whatever you want, but you're goin'. I can't put you on the street without you seein' him."

"The ranger is still looking into the shooting."

"So. Don't back-talk me, boy. You do as your told. Now, get outta here. And close my door."

Jimmy shut the door a little harder than he intended. He walked from the building to the parking lot. Collins pulled in as Jimmy was unlocking his car. He waited for Collins to get out.

"That doctor you seen after your shooting last year, who was it?" Jimmy asked.

"Sawyer," Mike said, walking over to where Jimmy stood by his car, "Why?"

"I gotta go see him today."

"He's a good one."

Jimmy grumbled and got in the car, driving off leaving Mike standing in the lot. Jimmy was driving faster than he should, grumbling and talking to himself. When he arrived at the clinic, he stared at the building.

Taking a deep breath, he got out and walked in. After sitting in the lobby for just a few minutes, he was called back to the doctor's office.

Doctor Don Sawyer's office door was standing open, so Jimmy knocked on the door frame. Sawyer motioned for him to come in. As he stood to introduce himself, walking around the desk, Jimmy saw he was a big guy. He was about the same height as Jimmy at six-foot four inches, but heavier, around three hundred pounds. None of it was fat it seemed. The doctor closed the door after introductions and motioned for Jimmy to sit down.

"Now. I know you're going to say you're fine. I hear it every time from everyone. But maybe you aren't so fine as you think," Sawyer said, as an opening statement.

"The shooting was a good one. He had a knife he attacked me with after he nearly killed his girlfriend. So, yeah, I think I'm okay with that."

"What are you not okay with then?" Sawyer asked, shifting his weight in the oversized chair.

Jimmy hesitated, then he figured he was not getting out without talking about something. "I found out this mornin' that all my career plans may be in doubt because of this shooting."

"How?"

"For a few years now, it was decided that I was to be the next chief of police. Now a councilwoman is casting doubt on that decision as well as trying to run my boss off," Jimmy said, starting to feel relaxed with this stranger.

Jimmy explained to the doctor everything. He told him how the drugs in Ridney's system could have made him act like he did to get shot and how his shooting could possibly be connected to at least one other case of an officer attack in the city.

Jimmy said more than he thought he would and talked longer than he would have guessed he would, but he felt better for having done so. He took a deep breath and rubbed his hand across his face.

"I don't want my career derailed because of a politician who has no credibility," Jimmy said.

"Maybe, lieutenant, you can enhance your credibility by finding the reason for these attacks."

Chapter 20

B.J. Tolliver was hoping for silence while working on monthly reports when he became aware of a person standing in his doorway.

Looking up, he saw the DPS narcotics investigator Robert Weeps standing there holding a file folder.

"You gonna come in or just lurk in my doorway?" Tolliver said, removing his reading glasses and leaning back in his chair.

"You may have a problem," Weeps said, sitting in one of the chairs in front of the chief's desk.

"You gonna tell me or do I need to start guessing?"

"The meth y'all found yesterday and the meth found in Ridney's system all had the same characteristics. Methamphetamine mixed with bath salt. Now, either your two tweakers were hanging around each other sharing their dope or someone in the area is sellin' bad drugs."

"You didn't make that jump with just two cases."

"No sir. The sheriff's office has had several cases of known users acting like superman when they dealt with them lately. The other city police in the county have had dealings with meth heads causing harm. For instance, the county had a guy they arrested for trying to hump a tree, naked."

"Same dope mix?" Tolliver asked.

"Yes sir. I had the lab analyze all the dope in question today and compare it with other samples from this area. It's preliminary, but my tech says it's the same basic mixture. Someone is intentionally selling bad meth."

"You goin' to stick around and help us out? I feel I am out of my depth here."

"My lieutenant has given me permission to help you guys where I can."

"Fine. Let me call my captain and have him work with you and coordinate with patrol what you need." Tolliver picked up the phone and dialed the extension telling Morgan to come to his office.

"Captain Jim Morgan, DPS narcotic investigator Robert Weeps. He has some information on the dope we been findin' lately. So both of you know, I sent Collins to the hospital to talk to the Perkins girl again. He will be back shortly, I'm sure. I would like him involved as much as possible."

Weeps looked at Tolliver and Morgan, "Sure. The more the merrier. Right now, maybe me and your captain can go over who sells in town."

"We don't really know. We hear rumors but we have no proof. We don't have a full-time drug unit. Patrol does most of our drug investigations," Morgan said.

"Is that effective?" Weeps asked.

"No. It isn't. But we don't have the manpower or the budget for long-term, full length drug investigations," Tolliver said.

"The county help in anyway?"

"We don't get along with the county much." Morgan said, not adding anything else.

That was the way some agencies operated. The county and city did not cooperate at the upper brass level, but the street officers work together well. Tolliver had seen it both ways in his years. Now it seemed the county and city were at a great divide where the county officials felt that Tolliver was set in his ways and not advancing with the times.

Tolliver felt his job was as a peacekeeper, a lawman, not some political figure trying to curry favor with the big shots of the day.

"Well, be that as it may, if we have some fool selling dangerous meth, which seems like an oxymoron to me, we will work to find who's doing it. Whether county or city," Tolliver said, standing, indicating to Morgan he should take his new friend to his own office.

Morgan and Weeps walked out as Tolliver gathered his things to go home for the evening. He glanced at his watch. Five thirty. He was going home earlier and earlier now days.

He thought about staying a little longer but decided against it. He turned off the light in his office and closed the door.

Chapter 21

Mike Collins walked into the hallway of the police station and could hear voices coming from Morgan's office. He walked to the open door and peeked inside. Morgan had a stranger in his office talking about drugs.

"Mike, meet Robert Weeps with DPS. Weeps, Mike Collins."

Mike shook hands with the man as Morgan filled him in on what Weeps had discovered during the day.

"I just met with Brenda Perkins again. She gave me the name of Sheehan. I don't recognize that name."

"Let's go to the jail and talk to this other guy," Weeps looked down at his notes, "Springer."

They all took separate vehicles for the six-mile drive to the county jail building. It was a single-story red brick structure that took up a large swath of land. It was enormous inside and housed the worst population of the county. If an honest check of the jail roster were ever conducted, most of the population in jail would be there for drug related offenses. Even the thieves and burglars were in jail for trying to supply a drug habit.

Inside, the jailer on duty buzzed them into a conference room. It had cheap cabinets along one wall and a cement table in the center of the room with cement seats fashioned after bar stools along the sides of the table.

The cops remained standing. After a few minutes, the inner door buzzed. Mike recognized the man as the one Amy had wrestled with yesterday. He was a short man, probably five foot three, and maybe weighed a hundred and twenty pounds. He looked sickly thin. Typical meth user look. Morgan made the introductions and read the Miranda rights to him from a form. Springer signed the form then started to apologize for his behavior, but Weeps cut him off.

"Look, save the repentance for later when you're in jail house church. We want to know the name of the guy you bought the dope from."

"I can't tell y'all that. I ain't a snitch."

"You got some kind of code you live by?" Morgan asked.

"Yeah, I guess. I know it don't involve ratting on people," Springer said, running his finger inside the grooves that had been carved out of the cement tabletop.

"How's your code feel about being lied to and nearly killed?" Weeps asked.

Springer looked up. "Meanin'?"

"You were sold bad dope. It was laced with a substance that caused you to act like you did. Hell, you're lucky to be alive. Are you going to protect the man who sold that mess to you?" Morgan asked.

Springer continued to run his finger in the carvings on the table and think about what was said. Mike and the other two maintained silence. Often in interviews with suspects, silence was a cop's best ally. Springer looked up finally.

"It wasn't a man. I bought it from a girl. She said it was new to the area. Better than what we had been getting." Springer looked at Mike, "Tell your girlfriend I didn't mean to fight with her yesterday."

Mike stood stoic not saying a word. How many people knew about him and Amy? He pushed the thought away, and asked, "What girl?"

"Her name is Mouse. I don't know her real name."

Morgan gave Springer the statement form he had signed earlier and asked him to write down what he just told them. After he was finished, they thanked him for his time and left the jail.

In the parking lot Morgan and Weeps looked over at Mike noticing the look on his face. They started laughing. Mike did not.

Chapter 22

Jimmy Williams left the doctor's office feeling better than he thought he would. He was reluctant to talk to Doctor Sawyer, but as he did, he began to open up and talk openly about his problems. Jimmy did not think he had anything to be worried about in his personal life, but the thought of a council member not thinking he was good enough to be chief, as had been planned for some time now, rankled him.

He was unaware how much he wanted to be the next chief of police until Tolliver had told him today that it was in doubt. He did not want to go too far with these thoughts because no one knew when Tolliver was going to retire. He also did not want to ignore it until it was too late either. He picked up his cell phone looking for the number to the mayor.

Jimmy asked for permission to drop by and see him. The mayor said he would be waiting. Jimmy had known Mayor Bob Montgomery since he was a kid. He worked for him hauling hay and working cattle in high school. It was Montgomery that told Jimmy, after his football injury, that he should go the academy and be a police officer. Montgomery was close to eighty now but still had a sharp mind and was always good for advice when Jimmy needed.

He knocked on the front door of the modest wood frame house Montgomery lived in on the edge of the city. Melva Montgomery answered the door and invited him in. She seemed to be like everyone's grandmother in town. She loved Colby and her circle of people in Colby loved her. Like most, the Montgomery's did not see the bad side of the city. She led Jimmy to a bedroom that had been converted to an office where the Mayor did most of his work from since the city did not provide an office for the mayor.

"Jimmy, come in," Montgomery said, offering a chair.

Jimmy sat and sighed, "How you doin' Mister Montgomery?"

"I'm fine. Heard about your dance with that man downtown. You okay?"

Jimmy grinned at the Mayor's phrasing, "Yeah. Wanted to talk to you about Janet Long."

"Oh, what about Janet?"

Jimmy filled him in on her visit to Tolliver this morning. He told him about her threats to Tolliver being witnessed and about her not wanting Jimmy as chief. When he finished Montgomery was silent for a bit.

"She's one voice, son."

"I know, sir, but I don't want her voice to gain any volume. You know what I mean?"

The Mayor nodded, "I wouldn't worry. Has B.J. said when he's gonna retire?"

"Not that I know of."

"Well, it can't be soon enough. I like B.J., but I'd like to see you in that office before I die."

"Sir, I really don't want to bash the chief. He's been real good to me. I just want your advice on how to handle Miss Long."

Montgomery laughed, "How do you handle jock itch? You keep applyin' salve and scratch it when you have to."

"What?" Jimmy asked.

Montgomery did not expand on his non answer. Instead, he invited Jimmy to stay for supper. Jimmy declined the offer.

In his pickup he thought of Mayor Montgomery and his questions about Tolliver. Why would Montgomery be worried about the chief retiring? Montgomery was a solid supporter of Tolliver's going back decades. Something was not feeling quite right.

Jimmy started his pickup, and as he pulled away from the curb, he glanced back at the house he just left. He thought he saw the front living room curtain move.

Chapter 23

B.J. Tolliver jerked his hand from the pan in the oven. His oven mitt was old and worn out and did not protect like it should. He grabbed the pan again and quickly sat it on the stove top. Chicken nuggets scattered off the pan. He looked at his fingers after removing the mitt. They were red but not blistered. He threw the offending oven mitt in the trash with zeal.

A knock on the door interrupted him. He glanced at the clock on the stove. Nearly six thirty. Much too late for visitors, he opened the door prepared to run off whoever it was.

"Oh, well, Jimmy. What are you doin'?"

"Chief, I need to talk to you about somethin'."

"Now? I was fixin' supper." Tolliver stepped aside and invited him into the small house. The front door opened into the living room and Jimmy stood just inside the doorway and sniffed.

"Chicken nuggets, again?"

"Yeah, well. You know."

Tolliver offered him a seat on the couch and Jimmy sat. Tolliver went back into the kitchen, retrieved the oven mitt from the trash, put the stray nuggets back on the pan, and placed the pan back in the oven to stay warm. He came back and sat in a hardback rocker in the corner.

"Chief, I just left Mayor Montgomery's house." Jimmy said, not saying anything else.

Tolliver raised an eyebrow, "Well, thanks for letting me know."

"I don't know what just happened over there."

"Well, tell me already, son."

"I went to ask his advice on how I should handle Janet Long. I got the feeling he knew more about her talking to you than he let on."

"Janet Long ain't your problem, yet," Tolliver said, annoyance in his voice.

"Chief, I was just talking to the Mayor as a man I have known and trusted my whole life."

"Then why are you here telling me."

"He asked me if you said anything about retiring, I said no, and he said it couldn't be soon enough. I get the feeling Miss Long has started her recruiting effort to remove you," Jimmy hesitated, "I don't want to see you pushed out of this job."

Tolliver stood, "Because you want to make sure you get it."

"No. Stay till you're eighty. I don't care." Jimmy could feel his anger growing as he stood. He was taller than the chief, but he always felt like a little kid talking to him. "I just want you to be careful of the council, that's all." Jimmy walked to the front door and opened it.

"Jimmy. Thanks for coming by. Let's keep each other informed on what we know."

Jimmy nodded then left the house. Tolliver stood there for a moment. Political games were always being played in small towns. In the past Tolliver had the energy to beat most people at their own games. Now he was not so sure.

He thought a lot today about what Janet Long had said this morning. He had been doing the job a long time. He pulled the nuggets out of the oven and started making a plate. Him and his wife had plans for retirement. If she were still alive, he would have probably retired already. She died six years ago. Damn aneurism.

Now the job was all he had it seemed. He and Joan never had kids, Joan couldn't, so they committed themselves to their jobs. She was a year away from retiring as a schoolteacher when she died. Now he wondered if his job was worth fighting for anymore. Another year or two wouldn't make a huge difference in the pension check, but staying for the money was wrong, too.

He squeezed ketchup on his plate and took a beer from the fridge. He sat on the couch in the same spot Jimmy had just been.

Chapter 24

Mike pulled his cellphone out of his pocket and called Amy Roberts. They agreed to meet at a convenience store to get coffee. When she pulled in the parking lot, Mike got out and met her at her car as she parked. He was frowning at her as she got out.

"Interviewed your boy Springer just now. He told me to tell my girlfriend he was sorry for fighting with her."

"What?" Amy said, wrinkling her face into a scowl, "How did he know that?"

"Morgan said there were no secrets in a small town. Guess not." They walked in the store to the coffee urns and filled Styrofoam cups.

"I want to go to poverty point and see if we can find a mailbox with the name Sheehan on it," Mike said. They walked out of the store as the clerk wished them a good day.

"You want to drive the entire point?" They stood by Mike's car now watching the people coming and going.

"You got a better way of findin' this Sheehan?"

"Jail records, water bill, Google." Amy said.

Mike was silent. He always seemed to take the hard way when looking for someone. He kept making rookie mistakes. This one was embarrassing because it happened in front of Amy.

"Okay, I'll call girl at the water department," Mike said.

In a few minutes he disconnected the call to the utilities and put his phone in his pocket.

"Address on Frost Street." He said.

They got in their cars, and Mike led the way to the address. The house was a wood frame house that needed paint. Other than that, it was one of the better houses in poverty point. The roof seemed newer, and all the windows were intact.

An old black man sat on the front porch in a rocking chair eyeing the police cars as they stopped in front of his house. He looked to be in his seventies if a day.

Mike got out and noticed there was no mailbox by the curb. This couldn't be the house Brenda Perkins told him about. He approached the elderly man in hopes of finding out.

"Evening sir, we are with the police," Mike said as introduction.

"Figured so y'all dressed like that. Too early for Halloween. What y'all doin' down here?"

"Looking for a man named Sheehan. Heard this was his address," Amy said.

"I'm Sheehan. Charles Sheehan. What you want with me? I ain't caused no trouble in decades."

"Well sir, this particular Sheehan is supposed to know about selling drugs," Mike said.

"I don't sell no drugs and any fool that says different is lyin'. I'm retired from the postal service. Got me a good pension, got my health, and got my wife. I ain't messin' with no drugs."

"You get your mail here? Noticed you ain't got a mailbox," Mike said.

"Mail goes to the post office. Why?"

"I think we got some bad information. This address popped in our system when we ran your last name in it," Amy said.

"My boy could of used this address when he was in trouble. Charles Junior. We call him Charlie. Now, he may be the drug dealer you're looking for. We fell out a while back over it," Sheehan said, shaking his head as he spoke.

"He live close?" Mike asked.

"Over on Edgewood."

Edgewood was down the street in the middle of poverty point. They thanked Charles Sheehan for his time and help. Mike and Amy walked back to their vehicles. Mike wanted to drive by Edgewood and see if there was a mailbox by the curb and if the Sheehan name was on it.

Chapter 25

The next morning B.J. Tolliver walked into the office a little later than normal. It was close to eight o'clock. He was usually always in his office for hours by this time. Today, he did not feel like coming to work at all.

He had a crowd waiting on him when he came in the hallway. Jimmy Williams, Jim Morgan, DPS investigator Robert Weeps, and Ranger Bart Murphy were sitting in the break room as he walked by. They all stood and followed him to his office.

"Why do I feel like y'all have been waitin' on me?" Tolliver asked, sitting at his desk.

The office was small as it was, and as everyone came in, the room seemed smaller.

"Chief, last night Roberts and Collins may have given us a solid lead on who is dealing," Morgan said, handing Tolliver a note, "This is what Collins left on my door after his shift last night."

Tolliver read the note then handed it back.

"Springer gave us the name of a girl, calls herself Mouse. Don't know her real name," Jimmy said.

Tolliver nodded. "Well, what are you goin' to do with that information?"

"Collins and Roberts didn't make contact at the house on Edgewood. We thought about going back over there and seeing what we can find out," Morgan said.

"I told Jimmy already. District Attorney is going to present this shooting to the Grand Jury next week. I have all I need turned in already," Murphy said.

"Fine. You went to the doctor yesterday?" Jimmy nodded, "I should get your release soon then."

"I have checked out other drug arrests for the last year in the county. The weird arrests where they acted crazy started in the last six months. It's been mostly in the county and over in the other cities. Seems it finally made its way here," Weeps said.

The intercom buzzed. There was a guest in the lobby to see Tolliver. He sighed as he stood. Everyone left his office as they came in, following him. He opened the door to the lobby and saw Mayor Bob Montgomery standing there. Tolliver invited him in. As Tolliver led the way to his office, he saw Jimmy give Montgomery a scornful look. Once seated, Montgomery did not exchange pleasantries.

"How long we known each other B.J.?"

"Many years."

"How many times have I defended you both as Mayor and as a citizen?"

"Are you looking for an exact number?" Tolliver said, leaning back in his chair.

"My point, B.J., is yesterday your officer stops by my house wanting me to dish dirt on a council member. Now, Janet Long has her issues with you, but she is popular with her voters. I can't alienate her like that."

"Maybe he came to talk to you, not as the Mayor, but as a man he has known since he was a little kid. A man he worked for, respected, trusted," Tolliver said, sitting up in his chair, making eye contact.

"Whatever the reason, makes me think maybe she's right. I don't know that he is cut out to be chief of police."

Jimmy was listening from the open door. He did not consider it eavesdropping since they were talking about him. Montgomery did not know he was standing there until he spoke.

"Well Mayor, we already got a good chief. I don't think he will be retiring anytime soon, and that suits me and the rest of us just fine."

Montgomery stood as Jimmy spoke looking from one to the other. Tolliver shrugged. Montgomery pushed past Jimmy without saying a word.

Chapter 26

Mike Collins sat at the Colby Diner waiting for his guest. He had called her last night and offered to buy her breakfast. It was almost eight thirty. She came through the door and spotted him. She waived. He stood as she approached and waited for her to sit down.

The last year had been a total makeover for her. She looked good, healthy, and happy.

"Mike. I was glad to get your call. It's been too long," she said.

They ordered when the waitress came. As she walked away, Mike looked at her for a minute then spoke.

"Been a couple of months. How's Lydia and Max?"

"Good."

Lydia was Christine's daughter. Max was her grandson. Christine Parks was not yet forty years old, but she'd had a rough life. The past year she pulled herself together. She quit drinking, she became a counselor for victims of abuse, and was going back to college for her degree. She helped the police department on cases of abuse, working with the victims. That was the reason for breakfast.

"You heard about the man Jimmy shot?"

"Yeah. Terrible," she said, sipping coffee.

"There's a female victim. The guy nearly killed her. She's putting the pieces together now in the hospital. I wanted to see if you could maybe talk to her and her grandmother."

"Absolutely. I would be happy to. What's her name?" she said, taking out a notepad and pen.

Mike told her the name and gave details of her injuries and the bad dope the man had been taking. Christine shook her head when he was done.

"That's interesting. In our group sessions some of the people talk about scoring from a girl. They said her dope was dangerous and makes you think your bulletproof."

"They give a name for this girl?" Mike asked, taking a forkful of eggs.

"Mouse. I think."

"Who told you that?" Mike asked.

"You know I can't tell you that part. These groups only work on trust."

"Worth a shot," he grinned.

It was good talking to Christine. They met under horrible circumstances, but it all worked out in the end. That case was probably the reason he and Amy had gotten together.

"How is Amy doing?" she asked.

"Good," he did not want to talk about Amy. Too many people knew about them already it seemed.

They finished eating and catching up on gossip. After they were through Mike paid the tab and Christine promised to go see Brenda Perkins later in the day. As he left the diner, he looked over at the police station down the block and across the street. Nothing going on there.

He got in his old pickup and pulled onto the street. His cellphone buzzed with a text message. It was Amy. He smiled just seeing the name. He opened the message. Chief wanted to see him. His smile faded.

He had worked evening last night with Amy, they had gotten in after two in the morning, and then he'd gotten up early to meet with Christine. Now the chief wanted to see him. He wanted a nap. He pulled into the parking lot of the station and got out. He was hoping the chief was in a good mood.

As he walked into the lobby, Jimmy Williams was walking out.

"Mike. Just who I wanted to see. Chief wants you to go with me."

Mike turned and followed Jimmy to his patrol car. He was not going to get to take a nap.

Chapter 27

Jimmy Williams led the way to his patrol unit as Mike Collins followed. Jimmy drove a few minutes in silence then looked at Collins.

"We are going to talk to Sheehan. Chief wants to know what he knows."

"No cars were there last night. We drove by twice," Mike said, yawning.

"As soon as we talk to him you can go back home. Or someone's home," Jimmy said, smirking.

"How did that scrote Springer know about me and Amy? Hell, how does anyone know?"

"Well, Amy is a pretty girl. Lots of guys would think so, scumbag or not. And rumors run fast in this town, too."

"You know Sheehan?" Mike asked, changing the subject.

"Not yet."

They pulled up to the house on Edgewood. There was an old Cutlass that would never be described as a classic parked in the driveway. In the yard was various old appliances, car parts, and trash strewn about. It looked like a dopers house. They got out and walked to the front door. Mike was watching for dogs or people. Jimmy's knock was loud.

The door opened. A woman stood in the doorway. Early forties maybe. Jimmy could not tell exactly. She might have been twenty.

"Ma'am, we are looking for Charlie Sheehan. He here?" Jimmy asked.

"Asleep. What's this about?"

"Can you get him please?"

She invited them in. For a moment Jimmy looked hesitant. No cop wanted to go into a house where the residents housekeeping abilities were in question. Jimmy led the way. They stood in a small living room waiting. The room was cluttered but clean. The house was already warm. It would be downright hot in a few hours.

"How can I help you?"

The young man was thin, sick thin. He was probably mid-twenties, but the years had been rough. His skinny chest was covered in tattoo. Some looked to be of the prison kind.

"Lieutenant Jimmy Williams. Officer Mike Collins. You Charlie?" The man nodded, wiping sleep from his eyes.

"Heard you were selling drugs."

"What? I ain't no drug dealer." He looked shocked to be accused of such a thing.

"You know a man named Tolly Ridney?"

"Knew him. Until you killed his ass."

"Girlfriend says you sold him the bad dope," Jimmy said, ignoring the barb.

"I work nightshift at the warehouse on Paxton. I ain't got time for no dope."

"You sell anything in the last few weeks? Remember, lying to us is a crime."

Sheehan's shoulders slumped, "Mouse had me move a little shit for her. But I only did it once. Sold it to Ridney."

"It was bad dope," Mike said.

"Ain't been around Mouse in a while. They set up, make a batch, then move."

"Set up where?" Jimmy asked.

"Anywhere. Last time was Crown Street in a boarded-up house. It's one of them flash lab things," Sheehan said, pulling a wife beater shirt on over his thin chest.

"A what?" Jimmy asked.

"You know, flash lab. Here one minute, then in a flash it's somewhere else."

"You know Mouse's real name?"

Sheehan said he did not know. Jimmy thanked him, and they left the house. In the truck Mike looked at the house before closing his door.

"Flash lab?" Mike said, looking at Jimmy.

"Yeah. Also called mobile lab."

Chapter 28

Chief Tolliver was sitting at his desk trying to finish the monthly reports. Interruptions were the norm of the day. Captain Morgan stuck his head in. Tolliver looked up.

"Chief, we need to go to a house on Crown Street. Jimmy just called. That's where he and Mike traced our drug lab to."

Tolliver sighed. He stood and gathered his things and followed Morgan to the parking lot. They took separate cars but arrived at the same time. Jimmy and Mike were already there looking in cracks of boarded up windows and standing around.

Tolliver walked up to them, "What are y'all doin'?"

"Sheehan said this was the house they made that bad meth in. Nobody's here though," Mike said.

"Probably not in a few weeks," Jimmy said.

"Sheehan said it was a mobile lab. They set up in an old house, make a batch, then move locations," Mike said, looking in the front window.

"Let's talk to the neighbors. See if they saw anything the last few days," Morgan said, walking across the street.

Tolliver nodded at Mike who followed Morgan.

"Jimmy, I think we need to go in. Make sure everything is okay."

"Yeah. Someone could be hurt in there."

"Sure. Kick that door in."

Jimmy kicked the old wooden door causing it to split in half. He grabbed the half with the doorknob and pushed it into the house. Tolliver followed him in the house.

"Stinks, huh?" Tolliver said. The chemical smell that lingers long after a meth lab is removed was strong.

They walked through the house avoiding the trash and broken glass pipes that were used to smoke meth. The floors had holes in them in places allowing a view to the ground outside. The ceiling was missing in places allowing a view to the underside of the roof. No evidence of a lab anywhere around.

"You said Sheehan said they move around."

"Yes sir."

"Well, how would Tolbert Ridney know to find wherever they are set up again. Someone had to communicate that to him and all the other customers," Tolliver said, kicking at a glass pipe.

"We got the name of a female pusher named Mouse. We don't know anything else about her," Jimmy said.

"So, they set up, make a batch of dope, and then move locations. Seems like a lot of work for a bunch of dopers. Why not do it the easier way. Where are they getting the chemicals to make this crap?" Tolliver asked.

They stepped back outside into the yard as Morgan and Collins walked up.

"Some neighbors aren't home, but those that are didn't see nothing," Morgan said.

Jimmy bent to pick something up from the overgrown flowerbed. He held it up to show the others.

"What is that?" Tolliver asked, taking it from Jimmy. He read it aloud, "The Horseshoe Bar."

Mike took it from the Chief. "Perkins mentioned that this Mouse girl worked there, and Tolbert Ridney hung out there."

"Well, maybe you and Jimmy ought to go see who else is hangin' out there," Tolliver said.

Chapter 29

Mike Collins and Jimmy Williams left the Crown Street house heading to the Horseshoe Bar. The bar was just outside the city limits by about two miles, but they had both helped the county deputies answer fight calls there in the past. Mike was hoping to find someone at the bar who knew about the meth dealers.

Jimmy was silent as he drove toward the bar. Mike could not take the silence any longer.

"What's wrong, Lieutenant?"

"Nothing," he said, shaking his head, then continued, "Just I ain't been sleeping that good."

"Dreams?"

"Yeah." Jimmy looked at Mike.

"I still have mine too," Mike said, "Doctor Sawyer says they get less frequent, but I don't know."

Jimmy pulled into the gravel lot of the bar. There were already about half a dozen cars in the lot despite it being just before noon. They parked, staring at the cinder block building with no windows. There was only a horseshoe shaped wood sign with the name of the bar on the front of the building. They got out and walked in through the heavy gray metal door that served as the front door.

It smelled of cigarette smoke and stale beer. The odor permeated everything inside. There was a female bartender behind the bar cleaning glasses. Her cigarette dangling from her lips had an ash that was held on by sheer luck. As they walked toward her the ash fell over the clean glasses. She did not wipe it off.

"Excuse me. We need your help," Mike said, careful not to lean on the scarred and scuffed bar.

"With what?" She asked.

"Looking for a girl called Mouse. You know her?" Jimmy asked looking at the girl's tattooed arms. They were stick thin, and the bends of both arms had needle tracks on them.

"Nope," she said, noticing Jimmy staring. "You never seen needle marks before?"

"Yeah. Wondering how fresh those are," Jimmy said.

"They're old."

Mike was unsure. For a drug addict, time meant nothing. Old to her might mean days or months.

"We're looking into some bad dope. People probably hang out here," Mike said.

"Thought all dope was bad. Lots of people hang out here," she said.

"What's your name?" Mike asked.

"Melanie Radinski."

"Melanie, this dope is meth laced with bath salt. I guess you know what that means, right?" Mike said.

"That's bad shit, huh? I can't help you. If you'll excuse me, I got work to do. You're welcome to come back tonight to check our guest list." She moved off down the bar line.

Outside in the clear air Mike looked at Jimmy, "Well?"

"Well, we go back to the chief and tell him that Melanie the bartender is lying about not knowing Mouse."

Mike nodded in approval. "You can do that. You drop me off. I got to meet someone this afternoon," he said.

Chapter 30

Chief Tolliver pulled into the parking lot of the station. He decided he wanted lunch and he was going to walk to the diner. As he pulled into the parking space, he noticed councilman Joe Rice standing there waiting on him. He did not want to visit with any politician today. He got out of the car.

"Joe, what brings you here?" Tolliver asked, shaking hands.

"Your meeting with Janet and the Mayor. It could have gone better, you know?"

"It went like it should."

"I find myself being the lone voice on keeping you in office. You acting like that to them makes it hard to defend you."

"I can defend myself from them."

They watched as a pickup pulled into the lot and found a space to park. Rice looked at Tolliver and continued, "I'm just giving fair warning. You may be on thin ice, unless something changes."

Tolliver was still watching the new arrival. Weeps got out of the pickup and walked toward them.

"Joe, I appreciate that. I really need to talk to this man here." Tolliver walked away leaving Joe Rice standing alone in the lot. Tolliver met Weeps in the middle of the parking lot.

"You hungry? Let's go get lunch."

Weeps agreed and walked with Tolliver to the diner.

"Got something to ask you. Mind you, I am not a dope cop. We found they may be using mobile labs in old buildings to make this stuff. Why? There are easier ways to make meth," Tolliver said as they walked.

"Who knows. The shake and bake method only makes a little. Maybe they want larger batches."

Tolliver was silent for a bit. Shake and bake meth is made in soda bottles and such. It is simpler than having a traditional meth lab, but the dangers are when you mix the chemicals. If the person does not remove the lid properly, the bottle can explode.

"So, they have a traditional cook lab with all the chemicals set up in abandoned houses, make what they need for the next few days, then move the lab for the next batch," Tolliver said.

"Kind of smart on the cook's part. They make all they need to sell for the next few days. Find another location and make another batch," Weeps said, holding the diner door open for them to enter.

"If it moves all the time, how do people know where to buy it?"

"The cooking would be done mobile fashion. The dealers are fixed. They pick it up from someone and they sell it. The dealers probably don't even know where the lab is."

The waitress took their order. As she walked away, Tolliver sipped his water.

"Got the name of a girl named Mouse as a seller. Jimmy and Mike are chasing a lead on her now."

"Good. All I got is the meth is nothing special. Seems to be made with battery acid though. And of course, laced with bath salt. I think whoever is making this is wanting to send a message."

"To who?" Tolliver asked.

"Meth heads maybe. This mixture will make you go out of your mind, as you have seen. It will also kill you stone cold dead with one shot. I think this is deliberate to cause people harm, not about making money."

Tolliver was silent as the food was served. Who in their right mind would knowingly sell bad drugs to their clients? It did not make a lot of sense to him. They ate in silence.

Chapter 31

After Jimmy Williams dropped him off at the police station, Mike drove to the hospital to meet with Christine Parks. She wanted him to introduce her to Brenda Perkins instead of Christine just popping in and trying to talk to her cold. Mike agreed.

He met her in the lobby. As they walked to the hospital room together, Christine stopped before entering the room and looked at Mike.

"I hope I didn't pull you away from anything."

"No. I got called in to help on something after we met. I gotta be on duty at four."

"No rest for the busy, huh? Tell me more about this girl."

Mike gave her the details on Brenda Perkins. He concluded that she may know the name and location of the possible pusher named Mouse.

"Well, I'll ask if I can. I won't force it."

"I don't expect you to. I wanted you to help this girl. I feel she has had a shitty life."

Christine opened the hospital room door and entered slowly with Mike right behind her. Perkins was lying in bed staring at the ceiling. The room was tomb quiet. Christine made a quiet noise inside that Mike barely heard as she saw Perkins for the first time. Perkins was the only patient and did not have the television on. Her head was still wrapped in the thick bandage, and her face seemed to be healing as the bruising was different shades of purple now. She looked at them as they walked in.

"Hi." She managed to say, speaking a little clearer than she had the days before.

"Brenda Perkins, this is Christine Parks. You wanted me to find you someone to talk to who wasn't a preacher. She's it."

Perkins nodded, smiling a broken smile at Christine.

"I wanted Mike to introduce us before I just dropped in on you. Is now a good time to visit a little bit?" Christine asked. Perkins looked at Mike and raised her eyebrows, "Mike won't be staying. He has to find the person selling the drugs," Christine said.

Perkins nodded.

"I'll leave you two alone then," Mike said, patting Christine on the arm.

"Wait," Perkins said, slurring.

Mike looked around at her. She motioned for the notepad on the bedside table. Christine handed it and the pen to her. Perkins wrote something then showed it to Mike who read it aloud

'I lied about not knowing the cook.'

"Oh?"

Perkins wrote again, longer this time. She tore the sheet from the pad, folded it in half, and handed it to Mike. He took it.

"I'll read this in the car."

She nodded as a tear rolled from her blackened eye. Mike left.

He stood in the hallway for a moment. He unfolded the note and read what she had written.

'Tolly bought a lot of meth from Mouse. He also sold a lot of meth and marijuana for her. Tolly always said Mouse and her boyfriend were crazy. I don't know their names for real, but they hang out at the Horseshoe a lot.'

The Horseshoe again. He shook his head in frustration and walked out of the hospital. He and Jimmy had spoken to the bartender who said she did not know a Mouse. Mike glanced at his watch. He had to be on shift in an hour. Maybe him and Amy could check in on the night life of the Horseshoe and get some different answers tonight.

Chapter 32

Jimmy Williams got home a little after three in the afternoon. He checked the wall clock in the kitchen sighing heavily. He opened the fridge and got a bottle of beer, then grabbed a second bottle before closing the fridge door. He walked to his wood shop out back of the house.

He entered, turned the light on, and looked around. It had been a long time since he felt like working in here, as evidenced by the unfinished projects laying around. He opened his beer tossing the cap in the trash bucket by the door. He sat on the stool at the wood bench and took a long drink.

This cop life had taken a toll on him. He knew that. He did not need Doctor Sawyer to tell him that. He had seen and done things that left a man scarred and damaged for the rest of his life. He took another drink. He was not the only cop in the world who felt this way, so why was he being a wimp about it.

Mike Collins had shot two people just last year, and he did not fall apart. Chief Tolliver has been a cop for nearly half a century. That old man has seen some stuff in the old days that would make you have nightmares while wide awake. Jimmy took another drink, wiping a tear from his eye.

His stream of thoughts continued unabated. Why am I being so weak? I'm supposed to be the strong one. The star quarterback. The pride of Colby. That's how it was written in the paper when he signed with Texas Tech to play football there. He led the Red Raiders to a 7-5 record his sophomore year, but in Colby you would have thought he had won the Super Bowl.

The next season, early in the season, he was on the receiving end of a tackle by a linebacker that went on to the NFL. That hit had dislocated his throwing shoulder and ended his career. Then he lost his scholarship. He came back to Colby. Still the citizens treated him well, even if he felt like he let the city down.

Bob Montgomery, who was Mayor by then, had talked him in to joining the police force. Tolliver hired him and sent him to the academy. That was almost twenty years ago. He took another long drink emptying the beer bottle. He set it aside and opened his second beer.

His cellphone buzzed. Jimmy looked at the call screen. It was his mom. He did not feel like talking to anyone so he dismissed the call. He just wanted to be left alone. To stew in his own self-pity, he thought. In a few months he would be forty years old, but he felt he had nothing to show for it. No girlfriend, no hobbies to speak of, and maybe no future on the department. He wanted to be the chief. He somehow felt he was owed at least the chance to try and be chief.

He became aware of a shadow in the doorway. He glanced up. Chief Tolliver was standing in the doorway staring at him.

"I knocked on the front door. How long you been out here feelin' sorry for yourself?"

"I'm just sittin' alone, that's all," Jimmy said.

Jimmy tried to hide the beer he had opened. For a reason he could not explain if asked, he felt as if he were a kid caught drinking by his dad.

"That beer helpin' any?"

"No. I was just thinking about the mess I seemed to have made of myself."

"How so?" Tolliver asked, walking into the shop.

"Well, it seems I'm destined for failure. Failed at football, failed at every relationship I ever tried to have. Now, the future of my career."

"You made it farther playin' football than any other kid from here. Your career will be fine. It was a good shootin'. The D.A. will see it that way."

"The chief's job. Seems like a whole lot of alligators snapping at you right now."

"Yeah. We will get through that too. As far as I am concerned, you are the next chief. Now let's go get some dinner."

Jimmy sighed but followed Tolliver out of the shop. He felt better already.

Chapter 33

Mike Collins checked on duty by telephone instead of radio, as he was still getting his uniform on. He was running late. Nobody would care since he had been working today, but he did not like running behind.

His cellphone rang. It was Amy Roberts, probably wanting to know where he was. He ignored the call letting it go to voice mail. As he fitted the ballistic vest into place on his torso, he thought of Amy and smiled. She had made a major difference in his life. He thought of the sergeant slot he was unofficially offered by Chief Tolliver. He was determined to pass it up if he had to choose between the two.

He rushed out of the house; his cellphone forgotten on the dresser. He checked on duty by radio as he pulled out of the parking lot of his apartment building.

"Received 409. Be en route to 609 Crossway Street to meet 401." The dispatcher responded.

"10-4."

401 was Captain Morgan. Mike thought of what could be happening for him to need to meet the Captain there. He drove in the direction of the address without lights and sirens. As Mike turned onto the block, he saw several patrol cars, including Chief Tolliver's, parked in

front of the house. There was an ambulance parked in the street with the paramedics sitting inside.

Mike stopped and joined Amy Roberts, Captain Morgan, and Chief Tolliver in the front yard. Amy gave him a hard look as he approached.

"I tried calling you," she said.

"I was running late. Been a little busy today," he said.

"About to get busier. We got a body in there," Morgan said, nodding toward the house.

"Who?"

"We think it might be the female who lives here, a Myra Carter. We don't know for sure," Tolliver said.

"Why don't we know?" Mike asked.

"I'll show you," Morgan said, leading the way to the front steps.

Mike followed up the front steps and onto the narrow porch as Morgan stepped aside to let Mike look in the house. Blood was splattered on the walls. The blood spatter was so thick on the ceiling it was forming gruesome icicles. On the sofa was the body of what looked to be a female. The head was so severely beaten all that was left was a flattened mess with gore and brain matter congealing in a puddle in the sofa cushions. A five-pound sledgehammer was laying in the floor covered in blood and gore.

"We know who did this?" Mike asked.

"Her neighbor, Joel Rogers, did it. He was standing in the yard when I got here," Amy said, not staring at the body.

"Well, let's back out until forensics get here. I called Ranger Murphy," Tolliver said, as he stood in the front yard.

Mike followed silently as he thought of what he just saw. He caught a glimpse of the teenage boy sitting in the backseat of Amy's patrol car. Gore and blood hung from his face in little ribbons. He sat motionless in the car not looking at anyone.

"What happened?" Mike asked.

"All he said was 'she made fun of me'," Amy replied, not looking at the suspect.

Mike felt as if he was going to be sick.

Chapter 34

Jimmy Williams sat in his pickup in front of Mayor Bob Montgomery's house trying to find the courage to knock on the door. Last evening, the chief had been called in the middle of getting supper. He and the boys had worked late into the night at Myra Carter's murder scene. The rangers had been called, and after processing the scene all night, the forensics were collected. Now, it was a waiting game to understand why her neighbor had brutally killed her.

Jimmy had other things to think of right now. Mayor Montgomery was involved in something that did not seem right. His comments about Chief Tolliver retiring sooner rather than later were troubling. Montgomery was always a supporter of the chief. What had changed. Jimmy meant to find out.

He got out of the pickup and walked to the front door. He was sure Montgomery would be up by now even though it was not quite seven in the morning. His knock was answered by the mayor.

"Jimmy?"

"Mayor, we need to talk."

Montgomery stepped out on the porch, gently closing the front door.

"What did you mean the other day about Tolliver needing to hurry up and retire?"

"Not exactly what I said, Jimmy. Although, I guess it's close enough." He walked to the end of the porch and folded his arms around his body. He looked old and haggard like he was not getting enough sleep. He turned back toward Jimmy.

"Janet Long is out for blood and she is playing for keeps."

"She is just one person. You said she could be isolated."

"I was wrong. She is recruiting other council members. No, I won't say who. Just know it's a rolling tide right now."

"Why push him out now? He is close to retirement. Why not let him finish and walk away?"

"He has had ample opportunity to walk away. He hasn't. And Janet Long is not gonna let him now."

"Mayor, I don't understand this at all."

"Jimmy, you want to know why Janet Long has blood in her mouth for B.J.? Ask him. I cannot tell you his story."

"Where does that leave me?" Jimmy asked, staring at the mayor.

"I don't know. Janet Long doesn't like you, either. Now, excuse me, son." Montgomery walked back into the house, closing the door, leaving Jimmy on the porch.

Frustrated, Jimmy walked back to his pickup and drove away. What could possibly be the reason Janet Long did not like Chief Tolliver? She was the newest member of the city council, but maybe the grudge went beyond the professional level. Jimmy was unsure how to find out without directly asking the chief about her. He knew Tolliver would not talk about anything he didn't want to.

His first order was finding the drugs. If he could find where the dope was coming from and who the supplier was, he had a chance of isolating the chaos that was Janet Long.

Jimmy headed toward the office hoping to find someone to go with him to the Horseshoe Bar and confront the only lead they had, Melanie Radinski.

Chapter 35

Amy Roberts was completing a traffic stop, the fourth of her shift. The stopped was not having a good interaction with the stopper. She finished her part and gave the driver their copy of the citation.

As she settled back in her car, her radio broadcast loud feedback. The dispatch voice asked her to call the office. She activated her cell phone and called while sitting still.

"Yeah," she said when the dispatcher answered.

"County called. Bobby Springer wants to talk to you."

"Why?"

"I don't know. I am passin' it along."

Amy disconnected the call. She turned off her emergency lights and sat there for a minute. She headed back to the police department hoping to find someone she could talk to about this new situation.

She waited for a pickup to pull into the parking lot, and she followed. They parked next to each other and Amy recognized Lieutenant Williams. She got out and met him at his door.

"Jimmy, can I talk to you a minute?"

He got out, towering over her, and leaned against the front fender of his pickup.

"Bobby Springer wants to talk to me. County just called dispatch. I don't know if I want to go by myself. Should I?"

"I am tired of playin' second string on this case. I'll go with you to speak with Springer, but then you got to go with me."

Amy nodded, "Okay."

She drove in her car since she was on duty. Jimmy rode with her. The six-mile drive to the jail took just a few minutes.

At the jail, they were shown into an interview room with a conference table and comfortable office chairs that were located next to the multipurpose room.

Bobby Springer was already seated at a place at the table, no handcuffs, no restraints. Jimmy and Amy remained standing.

"You wanted to see me?"

"Yes. I wanted to apologize. And tell you something," Springer said, rubbing a yellowed, nicotine-stained finger under his nose.

"You got a lawyer, yet?" Amy asked.

"Don't need a lawyer to say sorry. Or to say I lied to the other cops. I know who you're lookin' for in all this."

He leaned forward with his forearms on the table and looked up at the two cops.

"Okay, who?"

"You accept my apology? I didn't know they sold me bad drugs. I smoke weed, mostly. Nobody goes psycho on weed."

"Is it important that I do? Tell me who I need to look for." She glanced at Jimmy who was staring at Springer.

"Nah, guess not," he sighed deeply, "You need to go find Mouse. She ain't hard to locate when you need a fix. She's at the Horseshoe Bar. I don't know her real name, but she's the hot bartender."

Chapter 36

B.J. Tolliver was sitting on the couch in his living room trying to decide if he wanted to watch TV. His opinion was there hadn't been a decent show on since Hee Haw, but he watched stuff now and then. The ringing telephone interrupted his thoughts.

He didn't have caller ID, so he had to answer it or let it go to the machine. He took pride in not being a slave to modern technology. He walked to the kitchen and answered it.

"Hello."

"Chief, Janet Long. I need to talk to you, soon."

"Ms. Long? What about?"

"The strange drug cases we have been seeing lately."

"Ms. Long, I don't know if us meeting is a good idea. We seem to not mesh well together."

"Chief, I ain't asking as a councilwoman. I am asking as a citizen to meet with the chief of police."

Tolliver looked at the wall clock above the kitchen sink hoping to find answers there. There was none. He sighed.

"Okay, where? When?"

"My office. Tonight. I'll be there around Eight O'clock."

"Fine."

Tolliver hung up, not believing for a second things were fine. He considered taking someone with him since he didn't trust Janet Long that much. He discarded the idea. She would have come to his office if she wanted everyone to know.

Her office was housed in a strip mall on the east end of the city. It had served as her campaign headquarters and now was her office. She worked long hours and was often found there.

He checked the time, a little under an hour until eight O'clock. Tolliver left the house a little before eight. The drive to Long's office would not take long. Besides, if he were late, it would do her good to wait a little bit.

Pulling into the empty lot of the strip mall, Tolliver parked in a space in front of her office. He saw a green sedan backed into a parking space about twenty yards away. He didn't recognize it. He didn't see Long's car either. She drove a blue Honda.

He sighed as he got out of his car, thinking Long would make him wait when he wanted her to be the one waiting.

He walked to the glass door to see if it was locked. It pulled open. It was dark in the lobby area. He could see a faint light from the office Long used.

He announced himself. Silence greeted him. Fully annoyed now, Tolliver walked to the source of the light and entered the office.

The office was a mess. Papers scattered everywhere and one chair turned over. He scanned the small room quickly as he stepped behind the large wooden desk.

Janet Long lay unmoving on the floor in her own blood. He knelt checking for a pulse. Finding one, he made his way to the lobby and called the office for EMS and an officer.

Chapter 37

Amy Roberts and Jimmy Williams were driving back to the police department when the dispatcher called for her. She picked up the microphone and responded.

"Go ahead."

"408 be advised 400 requests your response to 609 Broad Street, unit 4 reference an assault."

She acknowledged and looked at Jimmy.

"Wanna go?"

"Sure. Who did the chief beat up now?" he laughed.

"We will find out."

She steered into the parking lot and found the proper unit. She parked next to Tolliver's Jeep Cherokee which had an ambulance parked long ways on the other side of it.

They met Tolliver out on the sidewalk. He looked at Jimmy but spoke to Amy.

"It's a mess in there. A struggle. Janet Long got knocked in the head pretty hard, I'd say. EMS got her inside the ambulance now."

"I'll get my crime kit," Amy said, going to get the crime scene kit from the trunk of the patrol car.

"How'd you find her?" Jimmy asked.

"I was to meet her at eight. I was little late. Door was opened, room was dark, except her office. Found her in the floor, unconscious."

"Meet with her. Why?"

"She didn't say, except she had information on the drug thing we are working on."

Amy returned to the join the two with her Sirchie crime scene kit in her left hand. The small black box contained fingerprint powder, tape, and index cards for processing crime scenes. In her right hand was a tackle box containing latex gloves, sterile swabs, and a point-and-shoot digital camera for photos.

"We talked to Bobby Springer just now. He told us the bartender at the Horseshoe was our dealer, Mouse. We were going to go talk to her when this call dropped," Amy said.

"You process the scene, then find out where I am. Me and Jimmy will go find Mouse."

Amy went inside to get started feeling perturbed that she was not getting to follow up on her lead. She began taking photos starting at the front entrance. This was going to take several hours.

Chapter 38

Jimmy and Tolliver headed in Tolliver's vehicle to the hospital. Tolliver decided he wanted to ask Long about the attack first.

"Drop me at the hospital. Have Amy pick you up and y'all go chase down this lead she found."

They walked into the hospital together and made their way into the emergency room. It wasn't too busy tonight. Long was the only patient. They had her behind a screen and were working on her.

Tolliver told a nurse to let him know when she could talk to him. He led Jimmy to the waiting room.

"Go. I'll wait here, make sure she's alright for her to talk to me."

"You worried about her, Chief?"

"She may be a pain in my rear, but she didn't deserve what happened to her."

Jimmy walked out to the parking lot and called Amy to pick him up at the hospital when she was finished with the scene.

An hour later Amy pulled into the lot, Jimmy walked out and got in the car. It was nearly ten O'clock according to the dash clock. They had to hurry if they were to find Mouse at the bar. Amy drove faster than she should have to get there in a timely manner.

"How are we goin' to approach this, Lieutenant?"

"With hostility," Jimmy said, getting out and leading the way into the bar.

It was not a busy night at the Horseshoe Bar and Grill, but still the cigarette smoke hung thick in the air. The smell of stale beer and cigarettes was enough to make you choke. If the place had an exhaust system, it must have quit working sometime last century.

Jimmy walked through the haze to the bar. The bartender looked up. Melanie Radinski smiled a jagged tooth smile at Jimmy from the other end of the bar.

"Is that what Springer described as the hot bartender?" Amy asked.

"Taste is all in his mouth, I guess."

"What'll it be?" Radinski said, standing in front of them.

"Answers mostly," Jimmy said.

"About?"

"Why you lied about knowin' a girl named Mouse?"

"I didn't…"

"Hush. This officer is goin' to put handcuffs on you, then we are goin' to the station to talk."

Amy moved behind the bar to take custody of Radinski.

"If I refuse?"

"You refuse, I will get a warrant to search this place and make sure your permits are in order. That search could take days, a place this size," Jimmy said, looking around the bar.

"No cuffs."

"Yes cuffs. Policy. Chief will be mad if we break policy," Amy said, snapping the cuffs on Radinski's skinny wrists.

Chapter 39

Tolliver waited for about two hours before the emergency room doctor would let him see Janet Long. She was in a private room at the end of the north hall. The room was cool, and Long laid in the bed with a bandage on her head.

Tolliver opened the door, quietly walking in her room. Janet Long was awake. She looked over at Tolliver.

"Who found me?" she asked, trying to sit up straight in the bed.

"I did. I was late about five minutes or so."

"Thanks."

"I wasn't in time to see anyone. Did you see who did this?"

"No. I heard the front door open, thought it was you. A guy walked in and began hitting me. I can't remember what he looked like."

"You had somethin' to tell me about the drug case we are workin' on. You want to tell me now?"

"Seems silly to say it now."

Tolliver waited in silence.

"The bad drugs are supposedly coming from a couple that work at the Horseshoe. I overheard this at the café today. Couple of kids were talking."

Tolliver pulled the visitor chair closer and sat down.

"Now Janet, I don't believe that for a minute. You heard that at the café. You coulda stopped at the office and told me that. Or, told me on the phone this evening. Not made a special appointment to see me at your office. Let's have the truth."

"Too much between us, Chief. I am afraid of the repercussions."

"We have a long and sad history. But nobody should be attacked the way you were tonight. If our history shows anything, it shows you know I'll do my job, wherever it leads."

Long was quiet for a moment. Tolliver thought she had fallen asleep. He raised up in the chair to check on her. She looked at him, tears in her eyes.

"I don't know who beat me up. I never seen him before. But I think my son is involved in this dope dealing."

Tolliver sank back in the chair.

"Your son, Phillip?"

"I found some drugs in his room. I questioned him about where he got it. He argued. He left the house this afternoon around three.

"Phillip is all I have since you took…" She began crying fully then.

Tolliver offered her a tissue hoping she would not drag up ancient history. He needed to find Phillip tonight.

"Where would Phillip go?"

"The Horseshoe probably. He's there a lot," she said, wiping her eyes with the tissue.

Tolliver stood to leave. Janet grabbed his arm.

"Chief, please don't do to him what you did to my husband."

"Your husband did that to himself. That's what I have been tellin' you for twenty-eight years. I have to go find your son."

Chapter 40

Mike Collins was in the squad room getting his shift started when Jimmy and Amy brought the skinny bartender into the office area. The smell of cigarettes and alcohol wafted from her filling the room with foul odors.

Amy looked at Mike and smiled as they went past. They put Radinski, still handcuffed, in the conference room, then closed the door to leave her there alone.

Jimmy walked into the patrol room followed by Amy. They sat down and both sighed. Mike looked at each of them.

"Hard day," he said.

"That's Mouse," Amy said, stretching in her chair.

"No kidding?"

"Yeah, hard for me to believe she's the brains behind this whole thing, though," Jimmy said.

Mike's cellphone rang. He checked the ID. It was the chief. He frowned then answered.

"Yeah, Chief."

He listened a few seconds then disconnected the call.

"Y'all had a busy night. Long gettin' beat up, bringin' in Radinski. Now Chief wants me to go find Phillip Long. He may know somethin' about all this."

"Phillip?" Jimmy said.

"Yep," Mike said, standing up.

"Amy, can you watch her? Phillip can be cantankerous," Jimmy said, standing also.

Mike and Jimmy left the station leaving Amy to watch the bartender. They would talk to her when they got back. In Mike's car, they rode in silence to the Horseshoe to see if Phillip Long was there, even though the bar would be ready to close by then.

Jimmy had not remembered seeing Phillip in the bar, but he hadn't been looking for him specifically. He could have been one of the few patrons there. He said as much to Mike.

"If he ain't there, do you know where else to look? Chief seemed to indicate he was comin' to the office."

"Not really. I know I been up a while and my ass is kickin' at my heels. I wanna go home."

"Good luck with that. Won't be happening tonight. Who is Phillip Long?"

"Knot head mostly. In his early forties maybe. In and out of prison."

"Must be hard for Janet Long to have that kinda baggage."

"To hell with Janet Long. She wants the Chief out of a job so she can put her own man in. No sympathy for her."

"Yeah, but she did get bopped on the head tonight,

by somebody we don't know who is."

Jimmy grunted and said nothing more.

The only car in the bar parking lot was a green sedan. A check of the license plate returned expired to a name from Wichita Falls.

Mike exited the parking lot heading back toward Colby. It was going to be a long night.

Chapter 41

Tolliver came into the police department with Captain Jim Morgan following behind. Tolliver was surprised to see Amy still at the office so long after shift change. Amy explained that Mike and the Lieutenant went to look for Phillip Long.

"We will wait for them to get back before we talk to the girl. She said anything?"

"No, Chief. Not a word."

The door chime dinged from the outside entry door. Mike and Jimmy entered, looking at the crowd of people.

"We didn't find him at the bar," Jimmy said.

"Let's talk to this girl, see what she can tell us. Amy, this is your lead, join us," Tolliver said.

Mike left to go patrol and maybe find Phillip Long. The other four went to the conference room to talk to Radinski.

The room was rank with body odor, and the smell of sweat, booze, and cigarettes filled the enclosed room. Tolliver left the door opened as the others took seats around the table.

Melanie Radinski, in Tolliver's opinion, looked just like a tweeker should. Sick-skinny, scabs over both inner arms at the elbow, missing teeth, and a general unwashed appearance. She was young, probably middle twenties. Already a wasted life because of drugs.

"Where are you cookin' the drugs at now?" Tolliver asked.

"I'm a bartender."

"I know exactly what you are, you're in trouble. Got witnesses that say you're the person to see if you want to buy dope."

She looked at Morgan, "What's this fool talkin' about?"

"That's the Chief, be nice," he said.

"I'm lookin' for Phillip Long. Where is he?" Tolliver asked.

"Don't know him."

"Why do they call you Mouse? The way you look, Olive Oyl would be a better name," Tolliver said, referring to Popeye's cartoon girlfriend.

"Don't know what that means, old timer."

Amy decided she would ask a question, hoping she was not overstepping.

"We got a guy in jail that says you supplied all his drug needs. I'm sure the others we have in jail will talk soon. Get in front of this now and help yourself."

Radluski laughed hard. Looking around at the four cops, she laughed harder.

"Damn, girl. You gonna have to do better than that if

you want to break me. I ain't talkin'. I'm tired and I am going home unless you're arresting me. In that case, I want a lawyer."

"You're free. For now," Tolliver said, moving from the doorway where he had been standing.

Radinski walked out of the conference room followed by Tolliver and Jimmy. Outside in the parking lot, a green sedan was waiting. Radinski got in.

"That car was at the bar earlier," Jimmy said.

"That car was also parked outside the office of Janet Long when I found her."

"Tag comes back to a guy from Wichita Falls."

Tolliver looked at Jimmy, "Let's see who that guy is and how he knows our little mouse."

Chapter 42

Mike patrolled the streets all the while thinking of this Phillip Long. He didn't recognize the name. He figured he was a local, but he had never seen him. He wanted to find him for the chief. To show him he could be counted on.

It was after midnight. The only place open on this side of town for coffee was Smith's Market. The green sedan from the bar was the only car parked in the parking lot. Mike pulled behind it. Over the radio, he advised dispatch of his location and the vehicle's license plate number. He already knew it had an expired registration.

A man came walking out from the store. Mike stepped out of the patrol car to speak with him.

"Your car here is all kinds of out of date," Mike said, as he approached the skinny male subject.

The guy was acting nervous, looking from Mike to the car and back to Mike.

"I just bought it. I ain't had it long."

"You got a driver's license on ya?"

Mike shined his flashlight into the car's interior. He recognized Melanie Radinski inside.

The man was skinny and sick looking. He looked like all the other meth addicts Mike had encountered over the years: bad skin, stick thin, almost starved looking, twitchy, unable to stand still. He kept rubbing his arms and appeared to be sweating more than the night called for.

He gave his driver license to Mike. The picture did not look like the same person. The picture was a heavier, smiling man whose smile showed teeth that were forever gone. The name on the license was Mark Radinski.

"Let me check this," Mike said, going back to his car.

He asked dispatch for another unit to his location and ran the license check. A few seconds later he heard Amy acknowledge, heading his way.

Mike walked back to the man, who was leaning on his front fender staring into his car's interior shaking his head at his passenger.

"Your license is expired, your car is expired, and you have no insurance. What am I gonna find if I search this car?"

"You ain't gonna search. I don't consent to that," Radinski said, straightening from the fender.

"You're driving a rolling violation. I don't need consent."

Amy pulled into the parking lot and joined Mike.

"Get the female out of the car."

Mike pulled his handcuffs from the holder on his duty belt. He cuffed Radinski, who wanted to resist but didn't. Instead, he kept silent.

Amy got Melanie Radinski from the car and placed cuffs on her for the second time.

Amy led Melanie to the front of Mike's patrol car where Mark was already standing. Amy stood silent as Mike spoke.

"The cuffs are for your safety and ours. I am impoundin' your car for the violations we discussed. Neither of you have a valid license. What am I gonna find in there?"

The two Radinski's stood silent looking at the ground. Amy watched them for reaction as Mike began inventorying the car's contents for impound.

The car was a disaster area. It smelled of old cigarettes and food odors and some cheap air freshener that was losing the battle. The glove box was full of napkins from various drive throughs, and the door pockets were empty of anything interesting. Under the passenger seat a pair of dirty women's underwear was found. Mike made a mental note to wash his hands, even though he had gloves on.

It was in the console between the bucket seats buried under a ton of trash that he found a gallon-size Ziplock bag containing a crystalline substance. A whole lot of it. The bag was packed full and bulged on the sides. It was more meth than Mike had ever seen before in one place.

Mike raised out of the car holding the bag up for the couple to see.

"Y'all are under arrest."

Chapter 43

Amy picked up the bag of meth from the patrol desk with a gloved hand. It was heavy. The color was darker than the meth she usually saw. She was tired from working her shift then staying over to help, but she wasn't going home now.

The others who had already went home came drifting back in. Chief, Captain, and Lieutenant all came in and looked at the bag, none of them touching it.

Tolliver looked at Mike, "Make sure the lab checks for fingerprints on this bag."

"Yes, sir," Mike said, continuing to type on the computer, filling out the lab submission form.

"We need to talk to them. I am assuming they are separated," Morgan said.

"He is in the conference room. She is in the old interrogation room," Amy said.

The old interrogation room was basically a closet that was not big enough for suspects and cops to sit in together. It was hot. No air circulated. It had not been used in years. It was mostly used as a storeroom.

"Bring her to my office. Amy, use your body cam to record this interview. Sit it facing her on my desk before she gets in there."

Amy left to set up the room. Jimmy went to get Melanie Radinski from the interrogation room and brought her to the chief's office, where Tolliver, Amy, and Morgan were waiting.

She sat in the chair across from Tolliver. She looked around the room, then down at the floor.

"Look here. You and your boyfriend, husband, whatever he is, are in some kind of trouble," Tolliver said.

"I didn't do anything."

"We found enough meth on you both to send you away for the rest of your life," Amy said.

Morgan read her the Miranda Rights. She refused to sign the form.

"You want an attorney?" Tolliver asked.

"No."

"Let's start with why you and your man attacked a city councilwoman tonight in her office."

Radinski looked at Tolliver and laughed.

"I was at work. Your officers seen me there."

"So, that means Mark attacked her, huh?" Tolliver said.

She kept silent.

"You don't have to say a word. Sit there and act tough. You won't be so tough when you are charged for murder with that bad dope your sellin'," Tolliver said.

"I'm.." She stopped herself.

"What? Speak up," Jimmy said.

"It ain't what you think. I can't tell you more right now."

"You better hope your husband don't throw you under the bus first," Amy said.

"I'm done."

Tolliver looked at her a moment.

"Officer Roberts, take this person to the county jail."

Chapter 44

Jimmy Williams had a rough night trying to sleep after they talked to Melanie Radinski. He slept fitfully, unable to solve the riddle that kept running through his mind.

After Amy left to take Melanie Radinski to jail, the chief decided not to talk to Mark Radinski until this morning. Mike Collins was to get him to the police station before going off shift so the interview could be done on their turf.

Collins had made a good arrest on the Radinski's, having found over a pound and a half of methamphetamine. It had the same color as the bad meth they had found around town.

Jimmy pulled his boots on to go to the station. He tried in his mind to connect what they knew about the bad dope.

Myra Carter, the lady who was beat to death by her neighbor, was a true innocent in this mess. She was not mixed up in the dope life. Her neighbor, Joel Rogers, had used some of the meth, become paranoid, and killed her. Ranger Murphy was working that case. He hadn't talked to Murphy about the details, yet.

He pulled into the parking lot of the station, his mind

still trying to make the puzzle pieces fit.

Collins was just getting Radinski out of the sheriff's patrol car. The deputy had brought Radinski here for questioning.

Once inside, they put Radinski in the conference room again. He had had a shower at the jail, but Radinski still looked dirty, his arms marked with scars from needle tracks and prison tattoos.

Jimmy remembered that Melanie had done no real time, a little county time but not prison. Mark was the convict.

Tolliver and Morgan were going to handle this interview. Jimmy was just going to watch. Mike took his leave as soon as Radinski was settled in. After activating the video recorder and reading him his rights, Tolliver began the session.

"We have been up all night workin' on this case of yours."

"It's meth, simple possession. I'll be all right."

"It's manufacturing and delivery. With the weight and your past, your lookin' at spendin' the rest of your life in prison."

Radinski laughed, shaking his head.

"Also, the case of attackin' the city councilwoman last night," Tolliver said.

"I didn't do that."

"Sure you did. Listen, you think you got out of there without leavin' evidence behind. It's all been sent to the lab. The hair and fibers, you're toast."

"We have talked to Mouse all night. She was at work. So, we know she wasn't there. Why did you attack the councilwoman?" Morgan asked, hoping to bluff Radinski.

Radinski sat quiet for a long time. Jimmy could see him weighing his options, to keep quiet or save himself some agony and cooperate.

"Wasn't my idea. That woman never did nothin' to me. You want a statement. I'll tell you everything once that crazy bastard is in jail."

"Who?" Tolliver asked, not liking what he was hearing.

Radinski sat still for a long moment not looking at anyone. Jimmy was growing impatient.

"Who, dammit?" Jimmy asked, sitting up in his chair toward Radinski.

Tolliver cast a look at his Lieutenant but said nothing.

"Her son, Phil."

Chapter 45

Mike dropped Radinski off at the police station and decided to call Christine Parks to meet for breakfast. They agreed to meet at the hospital cafeteria.

She was at a table alone when he entered the cafeteria. He took a seat across from her.

"You look like crap," she said as a greeting.

He smiled, "I feel like it, too."

"I was looking forward to breakfast, but you need to go home and sleep."

"I will, I wanted to find out how Perkins is doin'?"

"She should get out of here in a few more days. She really understands how messed up her life was, and I think she's sincere in wanting to change it."

"That's a start."

He got up, getting a cup of coffee from the urn at the counter then came back.

"You said you had heard people talkin' about this girl, Mouse, the last time we talked."

"Yeah."

She listened as Mike explained he had arrested them last night, what he had found on them, and how they were talking to the male part of the group now.

"Have you heard anything else from your clients that

would help us in anyway?" Mike asked.

Christine shook her head.

"You think Brenda Perkins could know anything else?"

"No, Mike, I don't."

They sat in silence for a long while. Mike was hoping to break this case, but so far, he was lost in the weeds. He didn't know how all the pieces fit. There was still a lot to sift through.

"I'm goin' home. I need sleep."

He left Christine there with a promise to keep him updated if she learned anything new.

Chapter 46

Tolliver sat at his desk thinking back on what he had been told by Mike Radinski. He looked at the rap sheet on Radinski again. His nickname was Rat, according to the CCH. He had several charges for burglary and drug offenses, nothing violent. Until now.

Now he was looking at a felony charge that would send him away for ninety-nine years, plus the assault on Janet Long.

His wife, Mouse, hadn't told them anything yet. Maybe she would. Tolliver picked up her CCH.

She had never been a guest of the Texas Department of Criminal Justice. Only county charges. Her involvement with what was going on now would guarantee a long stay in TDCJ.

Tolliver got up and gathered his things. He needed to speak to Janet Long. She was still at the hospital as far as he knew. Jimmy, Morgan, and the rest of the dayshift were looking for Phillip Long. Radinski had given them the location he had been staying.

At the hospital, he asked for Long's room number from the desk nurse. He entered as quietly as he could. Janet Long was awake, watching a game show on TV, the volume low. She looked at Tolliver and sat up a little in bed.

"How you feelin'?"

"I should get to go home this afternoon," she said, straightening the thin blanket on the bed.

"Listen, I got somethin' to ask you, but first I want you to know we got the man who did this to you."

"You did," she said, looking up at Tolliver. "He say why on earth he would want to attack me?"

"That's what I need to ask. He says Phillip is behind the attack on you."

"What? My son. Are you crazy?" she said.

"You said the night this happened to you that he was involved with this dope case we are workin'. You said you found drugs in his room. Knowing that and the times in and out of prison, mostly in, especially his last stint for twelve years, makes me wonder if he ain't the brains behind this drug business goin' on."

"That's just crazy."

"You know where he is?"

"No, he stays with friends a lot."

"The boys are out lookin' for 'im. It might be best he turns himself in. His partners in this attack aren't goin' anywhere."

Long kept her silence. Tolliver decided she was through talking, he headed toward the door.

"Chief."

Tolliver turned, looking at her.

"He blames you for his father. I guess that's my fault maybe. He came home talkin' of gettin' even with you for his father, for sendin' him to prison. For everything."

Long started crying. Tolliver, shaking his head, left the room.

Chapter 47

Amy Roberts came in early for her evening shift. She was wanting to see what progress was made on the case and help however she could. The patrol room was vacant when she arrived.

She was gathering paperwork for the night when her cell phone rang. It was the chief. She answered, listened to the orders he gave her. She was to find Morgan and they were to go interview Melanie Radinski. She clicked off her cell phone. She drove to the jail to meet with Morgan.

At the jail, they were ushered into the multipurpose room with the concrete table. Melanie Radinski was led in by a jailer a few minutes later. She had showered, but still looked dirty and tired.

After the introductions, the Miranda Rights were read to her by Morgan. She waived her rights by signing the form.

"We talked to Rat," Morgan said.

Radinski looked from Amy to Morgan saying nothing.

"Y'all are a pair, huh, Rat and Mouse. Kinda feel like you're connected to each other. But you're gonna do your time all alone," Morgan said.

"She eye candy, or does she serve a purpose here?" Radinski stared at Amy while talking.

"I'm here to see if you'll talk to us about what happened," Amy said.

Radinski looked at Morgan and shook her head, laughing.

"You're thinkin' I'm just redneck trash who deserves what I get, aren't ya?"

"I'm thinking you are in some trouble and cooperating will help."

Radinski looked at Amy again, "I'll talk to you but not with him in the room."

Amy and Morgan exchanged looks, Morgan picked up his notebook and left. Amy, with her body camera recording the scene, was left alone with Radinski.

"He's gone now. Talk to me."

"I want to know about Rat. Where is he?"

"Here in jail. Probably goin' to prison for a long time."

"We aren't bad people. Drug users, sure, but we don't hurt nobody. Never have in the past at least."

"Can't say that anymore. That meth you and him have been sellin' is deadly. Makes people act like mad men."

"The attack on that councilwoman lady? That was not our idea. Rat, Mark, would never hurt someone like

155

that," She said, looking over Amy's shoulder at the gray wall at something only she could see.

She looked Amy in the eye, "Her son, Phil, is crazy. Older than us, just out of prison. Rat did time with him in Abilene."

"You're sayin' her son had something to do with the attack?"

"All of it. The dope, the bad recipe. The whole thing."

"Why push bad dope?"

"I don't know. Me and Rat aren't the only ones dealin' though. There are a few others around the county. It goes a lot farther than just us."

"Where is this Phil at now?"

"I don't know. Rat does, maybe."

Chapter 48

Jimmy Williams sat in his truck in the parking lot of the Sonic waiting on his food. He was tired, hungry, and mostly mad. There were a lot of loose ends that didn't make sense in this case.

He pulled his cellphone from his pocket and dialed the narcotics investigator, Weeps, phone number.

They agreed to meet in an hour at the Holiday Inn where Weeps was staying.

The hotel lobby was empty when Jimmy arrived. Weeps waved to him from the breakfast area, which was closed at this hour.

"Lieutenant, how can I help you?"

"I got a burr under my saddle I hope you can help me with."

"Sure, if I can," Weeps said.

"This dope, where did it come from? I looked online for other cases like this. No other areas have this combination of meth and bath salts."

"I don't know. I work narcotics all over the state. Ain't never seen this before."

Weeps listened as Jimmy explained the arrests of the Radinski's and how they were passing the blame onto

Phillip Long. Jimmy explained the best he could how everyone fit together: Long and Mark Radinski having done time together in TDC, how they met up again in Colby. Weeps was silent for a moment after Jimmy was finished talking.

"No way this recipe is a new trend in getting' high. This laced meth is dangerous, as you have seen firsthand."

"The question then is, what is the purpose? Bad business to kill your customers or have them kill someone else?" Jimmy asked.

Weeps nodded.

Jimmy left the hotel still feeling annoyed. It seemed all they were doing was collecting information from past events.

Chapter 49

Tolliver sat at his desk alone in his thoughts. Joyce, the assistant, stood in his doorway. He looked at her.

"Janet Long is comin' into the building," she said.

The outside door chime dinged announcing her arrival.

"Bring her back."

Joyce led Janet Long to Tolliver's office. Long refused offers from Joyce for water or anything. She sat in the chair in front of Tolliver. As she looked at him, tears began welling in her eyes.

"I have treated you so bad. You have every right to kick me out of here. I wouldn't blame you a bit," she said, wiping her eyes with her hand.

Tolliver gave her a tissue and sat quietly, wanting her to talk.

"I didn't want to believe you about Phil. I didn't think he would be involved in this."

She was working up to something, so he let her find her own way to tell it.

"Lot of history between us, B.J. None of it pretty. I hope to find your forgiveness in the next few minutes."

"I don't have the power of forgiveness, Janet. That's the Lord's job. I have enough to do with my own job. At least until I'm out of this office."

She looked at Tolliver, "Phil called me earlier. Told me he was not goin' back to prison. I asked why he would go to prison. He told me he had messed things up, but he wasn't the one to blame."

"It's a mess, alright. Where is Phil now?"

"He didn't tell me. He sounded scared. Said that the boss was supposed to have his back, but they all turned on each other."

"The boss?"

"I don't know what that meant."

"You know where he called from?"

Long shook her head. She wiped her eyes with the tissue and looked around the room.

"My husband was a good man. He didn't deserve how it ended. I blamed you for it, for years. I think I poisoned Phil with that rhetoric over the years. Phil was a kid, barely a teenager when Bob…"

"Janet, I tried to keep it from happenin'. I told you that the day it happened."

"I didn't think he would do that, B.J. How was I to raise a kid on my own. I guess I didn't do very well at that."

"Bob stole a lot of money by embezzling from his bank. He was the president, for cryin' out loud. You had a seemingly good life. I was told to bring him in by the chief at the time. I waited until you and the kid were gone, then went to the house."

Tolliver could see it in his mind as if it were yesterday. Bob Long knew why Tolliver, who was the captain then, was there. Tolliver did not want to be there.

Bob Long and Tolliver were friends, and the families were friends, going to the lake together during the summers. Fishing trips, vacations. They were always doing things together.

Bob greeted him at the door, inviting him into his house. As Tolliver explained why he was arresting his friend, Bob said he needed to use the bathroom before they went. Tolliver allowed it. A few seconds after the bathroom door closed, Tolliver heard the gunshot.

Bob Long had blown his brains out all over the bathroom. His body lay blocking the door to the room. The rest of the department was there by the time Janet and Phil arrived. Janet blamed Tolliver for Bob's death. She never wanted Tolliver to be chief and vowed to have him removed. For twenty-eight years.

Chapter 50

Amy and Morgan drove in silence. Amy was replaying what Mouse had told them. Rat had not wanted to talk to them, further adding to her frustration. Amy was convinced Mouse was lying about the son's involvement. She said as much to Morgan.

"I don't know. He went away years ago. Dope and burglary. He's a loser, mostly, who was in trouble all the time as a teen."

"You send him up?"

"No. That was someone else."

The conversation dried up as they reached the city limits. At the police station they met Jimmy in the parking lot. They told each other what they knew.

"Ain't a hell of a lot, is it?" Jimmy said, shaking his head.

"We need to find Long before he skips town," Amy said.

"He's too stupid to run. He will turn up," Jimmy told her.

Tolliver joined the three outside. He stood with them listening to the exchange.

"Janet Long was here earlier. She says she don't know where he is either," Tolliver said.

"She okay?" Amy asked.

"I don't know. What I do know is Phil Long is a danger. If he set this attack up like those rodents say, then he needs to be caught now. Any ideas on where to look?"

Silence greeted him in response. Amy felt the tension between the group.

"I'm on 'til midnight. Anywhere I should look?"

"I would suggest the city proper, but what do I know. Keep a watch on Long's house, as well. I'm goin' home. You hear anything more let me know," Tolliver said. They watched as he walked to his car and drove away.

"Maybe some of his friends know where to find Long at, like the Sheehan fella in poverty point," Jimmy said.

"I can knock on some doors of people we already talked to. Now that we got a name, they may want to cooperate," Amy said, shifting her duty belt to a better position.

"Call Mike in to help. Y'all keep an eye out tonight for him. You go to Sheehan, have Mike talk to that Springer guy in jail," Jimmy said.

With a game plan for the night, the group broke up. Jimmy and Morgan headed home, and Amy called Mike in early for his overnight shift.

She was feeling bad about having to call him in. She felt even worse after seeing him when he pulled into the parking lot half an hour later.

Mike was bleary eyed and looked as if he needed to sleep for a week. He looked rough. Amy said as much to him.

"Been a rough, few days. Tryin' to get Christine to tell me anything the Perkins girl may have told her."

"Chief wants us to find Phil Long."

"Where do we start?"

"Chief told me to start in the city, so take that for what it's worth. Wants me to talk to Sheehan and you to talk to Springer."

"You could've told me that on the phone," Mike said.

Chapter 51

Mike was half asleep in the patrol room when the chief walked in. Tolliver looked at him. Mike had his feet on the desk and was leaning back in his chair from the doorway.

"Rough night?"

"Rough week. I'm tired to the bone."

"Any luck last night?"

"No," Mike said, sitting up in his chair, rubbing his eyes, "Amy struck out talkin' to Sheehan, too. Nobody knows Phil Long or his whereabouts."

"Go home. Don't come back until you're supposed to."

Tolliver walked down the hall to his office. He sat at his desk replaying what he knew. It wasn't a lot. He heard the door chime ding then the door to the lobby open. In a moment Bart Murphy peeked around the corner. Tolliver tried to hide his frustration.

"Chief, what do you know?"

Murphy sat in the chair in front of the desk. Even at this early hour Murphy reeked of cigarette smoke.

"I should ask you that. How's the investigation?"

"Fine. D.A. will present the case to Grand Jury tomorrow. No problems expected. Witnesses agree your man saved that girl's life."

"We knew that. Listen, in your lookin' into Tolbert Ridney, did you come across the name Phillip Long?"

"No, never heard that name. He connected to the drug case Weeps was tellin' me about?"

Tolliver nodded. His office phone began ringing. He looked at it annoyed and checked his watch. Not yet eight, he answered the phone, listened, then hung up. He stood gathering his things.

"You goin' somewhere?" Murphy asked, standing also.

"You might as well come along, too. Got a body at the park in the bathroom," Tolliver said, leading the way to the parking lot.

Chapter 52

Jim Morgan was on his way to the office for his shift when dispatch advised him to go to the city park to meet the chief.

He knew it was going to be bad. Most cops have an internal gauge that alerts them when things go off routine. Morgan's gauge was redlined at the moment.

In the park, he saw the chief's car and Murphy's pickup sitting in front of the cinder block building that served as the restrooms for the park. Groaning, he parked beside them and got out. Tolliver met him outside.

"Young man in there, DRT," Tolliver said.

DRT, dead right there, was the chief's way of saying he was dead.

"Who?"

"Dunno. Saved the investigation for you. Drug stuff all around him though."

Morgan walked into the restroom. He was lying on the cement floor, curled in a fetal position with his knees curled up and his arms tucked around his chest.

He was wearing only a pair of jeans and old tennis shoes. No shirt. He was young, maybe late teens, and thin. Morgan didn't recognize him either.

He went to his pickup and retrieved his camera and crime scene kit. It may be an accidental overdose, but it would be worked like a homicide until the medical examiner told them different.

"J.P. is on his way," Tolliver said.

Morgan began taking photos from the outside of the building all the way to the body. After the photos were done, he collected all the drug evidence. The same-colored meth was lying beside him in a small baggie. He looked through the man's pockets hoping to find information. An identification card was stuffed in the back pocket of the jeans, no wallet. Nothing else was found.

John Willis would be seventeen forever. Morgan showed the card to Tolliver.

"Seventeen. Damn shame."

"Same discolored meth we have been finding lately," Morgan said.

"Noticed it. Murphy called Robert Weeps just now. He should be here in a few minutes as well. I don't know how that helps us, though."

"I'm going to finish this. I'll have the body sent to Lubbock. You want me to do notification?"

Next of kin would need to be told. It was one of the hardest parts of the job, and no cop ever wanted to do it.

"No, I'll do it," Tolliver said, looking at the address on the identification card.

Morgan went back to work. Times like this he wished he had chosen a different career.

Chapter 53

Jimmy Williams was feeling at odds. He knew he needed to be doing something productive, but he did not know what that was. He could not help with the actual investigation, but he should be able to help look for Phil Long.

No one had located him yet, and he was the one missing piece to the puzzle. Jimmy decided to head out and search for him. The ringing phone made him stop, breaking his momentum. The call display showed it was Christine Parks.

Jimmy answered, listened then disconnected. Christine wanted him to come out to her house and discuss the recent events.

A few minutes later, Jimmy parked in her front yard, as there was no driveway at her house in the country. She met him at the front porch. It had been a while since Jimmy had been to her house. The last time was not pleasant.

"Come in, Jimmy, please," she said as she held the door for him.

He entered the kitchen through the laundry room since the door they used as a front door was actually the back door. The house was clean and tidy, unlike the last time he had been in here. He turned to face Christine as he stood in front of the sink.

"Thanks for comin', Jimmy," Christine said as she poured a cup of coffee.

She raised the pot to Jimmy, who shook his head, "What did you need?"

"We known each other a long time, huh?"

"We go back a lot of years, third grade."

Christine sipped her coffee then exhaled,

"Mike keeps asking me if Brenda Perkins has said anything that could help with this case y'all are working. I tell him 'no' because I like this counseling gig. I will be finished with my degree in a few more months, and I hope to have a big impact on the problems in this town."

"I'm assuming you're fixin' to tell me somethin' I ain't suppose to hear," Jimmy said, stepping closer to Christine.

There was no denying she had made a major turnaround in her life. The thought of making her do something she was not comfortable with caused Jimmy a moment of pain. She had been through so much, she needed whatever happiness she could find. If she found it in helping others with their issues and being trusted by them to keep it confidential, then nobody had a right to destroy that.

"Look, I don't want you to tell me nothin'. We are lookin' for Phil Long now and we will find him. When we do, we will have most of the answers we need."

"Long is just the tip of the problem, Jimmy," she said as she sat her coffee cup down.

"We know there are a whole lot of people involved, like the Radinski's."

"I heard a name from someone. I won't tell who, even if forced. But I think you need to know."

"A name? How does this name fit in this?"

"Because from what I heard this person came up with this idea in order to make changes to the police department. I need to tell you this because I know what your goals are for your career," she said taking hold of Jimmy's hand.

"In high school we were so full of dreams. You were the star quarterback, and I was all messed up in my mind. I always wondered if you even knew I existed back then. Now, we are pushin' middle age, and I'm just glad I made it this far. But you, you still got plans, don't you?"

"Christine, high school was a long time ago. I knew you existed, but you had a reputation that will do nobody any good rehashing. Now, I'm as confused as I think I ever been. What are you talkin' about?"

"There's someone else involved besides Phil Long. The Long's and the chief have a bad history that I'm sure is the reason he is involved. He isn't smart enough to do this himself. The name I have is," she released Jimmy's hand and looked him straight on. "Joe Rice."

Chapter 54

Tolliver sat on his couch watching an old episode of Barney Miller. He found most police shows boring and far removed from the reality of police work, except this one. Captain Miller was the kind of boss he would have loved to have worked for.

He had been hired by Chief Williams when Tolliver was eighteen. He would be sixty-five in a few months. Time sure flew, but at the same time passed like molasses on a winter's morning.

He thought about his career while watching the goings-on of the ole' one-two on TV. He had served under fifteen different mayors, at least seven district attorneys he could not recall, and untold council members and had seen a lot of police officers come and go. Some, like Jimmy Williams or Morgan or Mike Collins, stayed and made a career in Colby. Most moved on to better paying, or maybe just plain better, departments.

Tolliver had done his best to be the best chief the city had ever had. He had spent twenty years on the force, and when he thought of retiring back then, the chief at the time left for a bigger department. Tolliver was the most experienced officer, so he got the interim chief position. Then it became a full-time appointment. That was twenty-five, no, twenty-six, years ago.

With his wife passing on, with no kids, and him pushing sixty-five, Tolliver sometimes only felt he had this job to look forward to. Even with that, he was thinking, seriously this time, of retiring. Finally, as his wife would have said if she were here.

A knock at the door interrupted his morose thoughts. Annoyed, Tolliver muted the TV and walked to the door.

"Jimmy? What's wrong now?"

"Chief, can I come in? I know you hate being bothered at home, but this is important," Jimmy said, as he walked into the living room without invite.

Tolliver stepped aside, letting him in, then closed the door. He motioned to the couch. Jimmy shook his head,

"No, I need to tell you what I learned, but I can't tell you how I learned it."

"Well, go ahead. You seem upset," Tolliver said, as he led the way into the kitchen from the living room.

"The man behind this whole bad meth stuff. It ain't Phil Long."

"Oh! Then who?" Tolliver leaned against the sink as he looked at his captain. He could see the strain and worry in his face.

"Joe Rice!"

"Oh, come on!" Tolliver turned in a circle throwing his hands in the air. He faced Jimmy again,

"The councilman? My friend, Joe Rice? How do you know that? Who told you that?"

"Chief, I can't tell you that. But if it's true, it makes a lot of sense. We all figured Long was not smart enough to come up with this himself," Jimmy said, trying to calm Tolliver down.

"Come up with what? Pushin' bad dope and killin' people? Seems just like what Long could do," Tolliver said.

"More than that, Chief. Wanting to hurt the department enough to force changes to be made. That's the whole plan, what I was told."

Tolliver kept his silence this time. He thought back to Rice showing up at the office that morning when this was just beginning. He seemed eager to help. He even warned Tolliver that Janet Long was on the warpath for his job and that she wanted to block Jimmy from the chief job as well.

Him and Janet had spoken in his office two days before. She seemed to have worked through what grudge she had been holding onto. Tolliver hoped that was still the case.

"Jimmy, we need to go talk to Joe Rice, now."

Chapter 55

Jimmy drove while Tolliver sat silent in the passenger seat of Jimmy's pickup. Why he wanted to ride with Jimmy instead of taking his own patrol car, Jimmy did not know.

"Let's see if he is still at his office in town," Tolliver said.

Jimmy nodded, then turned to head to downtown to the law office that Rice owned as his regular job. He pulled into a spot in front of the office building, which stood alone on the side street from downtown.

Inside they were greeted by his secretary, Melinda Wallace.

"Is Joe around, Melinda? We need to talk to him pretty bad," Jimmy asked in a calmer voice than he felt.

"No. Went home early yesterday and never showed today, Jimmy. Want me to call him?"

"No, no. We will go there. Thank you."

Inside the pickup, Tolliver stared out the window, silent for a moment.

"Let's go back to the office. I want everyone there that's been on this case."

Jimmy headed to the office as he called the dispatcher to relay the chief's message.

They all gathered in the chief's office to go over the case. Mike was leaning against the file cabinets, Morgan and Amy sat in the two chairs, and Jimmy leaned against the door jamb.

Jimmy brought the rest of the crew up to speed about Joe Rice being involved. Silence greeted him when he was done.

"Are we sure about this?" Mike asked.

"The person that told me this has no reason to lie," Jimmy said, not wanting to tell Mike who it was that told him.

Mike said, "So what do we actually know? A council member teamed up with a convict to sell deadly dope. Seems thin to me."

"We don't know where anybody is right now. If we find them maybe you can ask them what they were thinking," Morgan said.

Mike ignored the tone in the Captain's voice knowing everyone was on edge about this case.

"What now?" Amy said.

"Now we go home and start tomorrow. Maybe we will have better outlooks after some sleep," Tolliver said as he stood.

Nobody disagreed.

Chapter 56

Tolliver pulled his pickup into his driveway slowly. He sat there for a minute after killing the engine. Jim Rice was his closest friend. The thought of him being involved in this scheme was almost unbearable to him.

He got out of the pickup trying to find his house key.

"B.J. Can we talk?"

Scared, he almost dropped his keys. The voice belonged to Joe Rice. Tolliver looked around in the darkness trying to locate the source.

Rice stepped from the shadows by the garage. Tolliver waited.

"I need to talk to you, Billy Joe," Rice said.

He looked as if he had not slept in days. Usually a fastidious dresser, his clothes were wrinkled and disheveled.

Tolliver felt bad for his friend, "Let's go inside. We have a lot to discuss."

In the house Tolliver motioned to the couch and Rice sat down. Tolliver sat in the chair opposite.

"I messed up…"

Tolliver held up a hand, "Before you tell me anything, know I may have to arrest you."

"I figured that. I need to tell you this first, though," Rice said running his hands through his hair.

"This was supposed to be so easy. Make a little extra money, live on the wild side. Phil Long was supposed to make it and sell it, I was supposed to be the money guy. It all went to hell, quick. With my position on the council and with my law practice and title company, I could find abandoned properties for him to cook his meth in. We had an agreement, cook here but sell it out of town," Rice looked up at Tolliver. He started shaking his head.

"It all went off the rails. Long started selling bad batches of the stuff, started hurting people, making them crazy. Then he started selling here in Colby. He said he had a plan to get rid of you and shake up this city."

"Me?"

"He hates you. Blames you for his dad's death. I tried to tell him there were other things to consider. You would retire soon and not be a problem. He told me you never would retire, that you'd have to be forced out. I disagreed. By that time, he was too far gone. The whole thing is too far gone. Can't be stopped."

"He found out his mom had talked to you and was going to help you catch him. He attacked her in her own office. What kind of son does that," Rice said.

His eyes were full of tears and Tolliver thought he looked foolish. Rice stood and Tolliver stood with him.

Rice pulled a pistol from behind his back. Tolliver looked at the revolver, frowning.

"You gonna shoot me, now?" Tolliver asked.

Rice looked at the gun, "This isn't for you."

Rice put the gun to his head and pulled the trigger, blowing brain and blood all over the wall of the living room. Tolliver watched as Joe Rice fell to the floor, dead.

Chapter 57

Amy Roberts was the first officer on scene. Pulling in front of the house at the curb, she saw Chief Tolliver standing beside his pickup. As she approached, other units arrived including EMS. She walked up to Tolliver and stood in front of him. He looked at her.

"He shot himself all over my living room."

His voice sounded hollow.

"Did he say why?"

"He talked about Phil Long."

He looked past her, "Here comes Morgan now," he said.

Amy went to help EMS leaving them alone to talk. She went back to her patrol car and got her crime scene kit. She began working the crime scene starting with pictures.

About an hour later when the Justice of the Peace Bob Harkins arrived, she walked him through the scene so he could pronounce time of death. She could tell the old judge was not in a good mood.

"Well, he did it, huh?" he said.

"Looks like," Amy said.

She didn't like the old judge and didn't want to make conversation with him. She was saved by Morgan motioning her over to where he stood.

"How's the Chief?" she asked.

"He's okay. You have anything on Long?"

"No. I don't even know where to look," Amy said.

"According to what Rice told the Chief, Long is the one that started making the bad dope and went all in on trying to hurt the Chief by selling the stuff here."

"What else would he say, though. He doesn't want to look like the bad guy."

"He looks like one now. He was the police department's biggest supporter. This is going to look bad on us all if we don't find Phil Long fast," Morgan said.

Amy shrugged, "I don't even know where to look."

They watched as the funeral home rolled Joe Rice's body out of the house on a gurney.

Chapter 58

Mike Collins reported thirty minutes early for his shift. He was working evenings this time. He was feeling the strain of too much time on duty and not enough sleep. He had the pass down report from Amy about last night's events.

As tired as he was now, he was glad he missed that action. Still, Phil Long was out there somewhere. He had to know he was going away for the rest of his life when caught.

Gathering his gear for the night, Mike heard the front door chime go off. The hall door opened, and Chief Tolliver came in.

He looked like he'd had a rough night. Mike was not sure what to say to the boss but tried anyway.

"Hey, Chief. Sorry about your friend. You okay?"

Ignoring the question, Tolliver looked at Mike and motioned with his head.

"Come down here with me."

Mike followed the Chief to his office not sure what he was going to be told but figuring he wasn't going to like it.

Tolliver went behind his desk and opened the top drawer. Mike stood in front of the desk, waiting.

"I meant to make this a ceremony, but things have been crazy lately. Maybe we can do something later," Tolliver said handing Mike a set of Sergeant stripes.

"Chief, I appreciate this," Mike said taking them.

"Just do your best and take care of your people. That's all anyone ever has a right to demand of you. Remember that."

Mike held the stripes in his hands, he feared his smile was out of place considering the latest events. He could not stop though.

"I will look for Long tonight on shift," Mike said.

"Good. I'll be staying at Jimmy's until my place is back together."

"Any idea where to look?"

Tolliver walked around his desk back into the hallway heading for the door. Mike followed.

"None. He could be anywhere in the county. The Sheriff's Office has been looking for him, too."

In the parking lot, he watched Chief Tolliver get in his personal pickup and drive away. He looked again at the stripes he was holding in his hand. He smiled again. He had to call Amy and tell her. She would be excited, too.

Chapter 59

Tolliver did not want to go home, well at least to his temporary home. He and Jimmy Williams had decided that Tolliver could stay there while his house was being cleaned. A crew from Fort Worth was supposed to be there tomorrow to get started.

Now, he was feeling at odds. The words Joe Rice had said kept coming back to him, echoing in his mind. That he would never retire, would have to be forced out.

He had talked of retiring with Rice several times, but in the end, that was all it was. Talk. Being in the job for nearly fifty years was maybe long enough. He used to feel pride in his years of service but not so much now. It just seemed like a long time. He didn't devote as much time to the office as he used to. Not as hands-on with the day-to-day work as before. He shook his head trying to clear his thoughts.

He realized he was driving in circles. He decided to visit Janet Long for a moment. Maybe she had a lead on her son's location.

Janet opened her front door before Tolliver could knock. She invited him in. He came in slowly, feeling uncertain about being in her house with her. Old animosities may not die that quickly, he thought.

"Janet, I was hoping you knew where Phil was."

"I have no idea."

Tolliver told her about Rice killing himself. She listened silently, tears in her eyes, until he was through.

"That must have been awful for you, B.J. I can't imagine it."

"I need to find your son for a variety of reasons but mostly for these drug deaths. You understand?"

Janet turned her back to Tolliver, "Too much death, Billy Joe, too much death."

Hardly anyone called him by his full name anymore. It took Tolliver by surprise to hear it from Janet Long.

Turning to face Tolliver, she said, "Are you sure about Phillip's involvement in this mess?"

"Sure enough. I know what the Radinski's role in this was. Selling and delivery to their drug customers through the Horseshoe Bar.

"I know that Joe Rice was the money man who fronted for supplies and tools they needed. He also, according to what he told me, was the one who found the abandoned properties the dope was cooked in.

"Rice also told me the cook and the ringleader for the enterprise was Phillip."

Tears flowed freely down Janet's face as Tolliver told his story. He could see she was struggling with the idea of her son being responsible for all the destruction of the last few months.

Janet sighed, "Chief, if you can, take it easy on him when you bring him in. He's more than likely at the cabin out by the lake."

Chapter 60

Mike Collins dropped his cellphone getting it out of his shirt pocket. He cursed his luck. He had to pull his patrol unit over. Getting out, he retrieved the phone and checked the screen. One missed call from the Chief. He redialed.

He listened as the chief gave his orders then disconnected. Still stopped on the side of the street, Mike called Captain Morgan. Morgan said he would call the others.

Thirty minutes later they were all in the conference room. Seated around the table were Mike, Lieutenant Williams, the captain, and Amy Roberts. Chief Tolliver sat at the head of the table. Standing inside the doorway were Officer Franks and Jones.

The officers sat quiet until Tolliver finished his update from his visit to Janet Long.

"What's the plan?" Mike asked.

"We are going out to the Lake before it gets daylight tomorrow to get him. I called Ranger Murphy and DPS Weeps to meet us out there."

"We know which cabin on the lake, Chief?" Jimmy asked.

"North shore cabin. It don't belong to the Long's. It belongs to a Long friend of theirs. I got the number in my car."

Looking around the table, Jimmy said, "Only one road in and out of the north shore side of the lake. We need to watch the cabin so we will know he's there."

"Sergeant Collins, to whom do you want to assign that duty?" Captain Morgan asked.

Mike felt a rush of pride as he heard that title with his name officially for the first time.

"Franks can have watch until 2. I'll watch from then until daylight."

"Fine." Tolliver said, standing ready to leave.

Mike was proud his first order received no backlash from the others. He followed Tolliver out to the parking lot where the chief gave him and Franks the number of the cabin.

"Be careful, boys. Make sure you ain't seen."

Mike nodded, reminding himself that Long could be dangerous.

Chapter 61

Jimmy Williams walked into his house feeling excited and exhausted at the same time. They finally had a good lead on Phil Long. Collins and Franks were to make sure it was solid or not. The series of events that started with a woman getting beaten on a busy street would soon be over.

He pulled off his boots, changed into shorts, then looked for something to eat. His refrigerator was barren. He grabbed a beer instead and sat at the table drinking it.

His cellphone chirped. Looking at the call screen, he saw it was his mother. He ignored it. He sipped his beer.

He lost the taste for the beer, poured the remainder down the sink, then tossed the bottle in the trash. He went to his bedroom and got dressed again. He was hungry.

He grabbed his gun and badge and headed out to his pickup. Sunset was just minutes away. He stopped for the red light on Main Street, frustrated to get caught at it. He looked to his right across the intersection to the Commerce Street. They had a green light. He spotted a Nissan Pathfinder coming across the intersection. He looked at the driver. Adrenaline kicked in.

It looked to be Phil Long driving the car. Maybe. Jimmy had not seen Phil in a long time.

Figuring it was better to solve his curiosity, he decided to follow. He looked to make sure the intersection was clear then drove through the red light. He followed the Pathfinder.

Jimmy was in his personal vehicle, so he was not worried about being spotted. He followed the car until he stopped at the Dollar General. When the driver got out, Jimmy recognized him.

He took his cellphone and called dispatch.

Jimmy waited for Long to leave the parking lot then followed him again. Jimmy had no way, except by cellphone, to update dispatch since he had no police radio in his personal pickup. If they stopped again, he would call in.

Jimmy was trying to stay far enough behind to not to be suspicious, but Long was driving like a mad man. Cutting in and out of lanes, driving fast down the city streets. He made a series of turns that Jimmy feared would give away his actions.

Long looked in the rearview mirror for a moment too long. The Pathfinder increased speed. Jimmy knew he had been made. He increased his speed.

At the same time, he dialed dispatch again to give an update on what was happening. He stayed on the line with the dispatcher giving updates on their location as he drove.

Long swerved into the other lane and made a left turn without slowing. The Pathfinder kept its traction as Long increased speed. Following behind, Jimmy copied the movement. His pickup was lighter in the rear, it slid around, tires squealing, rubber from the tires smoking on the street.

Then they were out of the city. Businesses and traffic gave way to pastures and open road. Jimmy checked his speed, eighty miles per hour, and relayed it to the dispatcher, who was the definition of calm.

Jimmy did not feel that way. His heart was pounding, his breathing was shallow, and he had trouble focusing on the Pathfinder. He knew he was experiencing tunnel vision, but his efforts to counteract it were failing. No deep breaths were possible.

The dispatcher, Shirley, told Jimmy she had the calvary coming, including the Sheriff's Office.

Jimmy realized Long was leading him to Colby Lake.

He told Shirley this then disconnected the call.

Chapter 62

Mike Collins pushed the patrol car harder than he should have. When dispatch came on the radio that the lieutenant was chasing their main suspect, he got excited. He would finally get to see in person the man they had been chasing for weeks.

Now, exiting the city limits, he could see the taillights of a pickup up ahead. Farther on he could see another set of taillights. He knew this was Long and Jimmy.

Darkness was fast closing in as Mike picked up the radio mic and told dispatch he had the vehicles in sight. The chief's voice came over the radio in response.

"Jimmy has no radio in his truck. Be careful on your approach to this man. He could be armed, probably is."

There was a series of acknowledgements from others in the chase. Mike did not answer. He was focused on the vehicles in front of him. He was gaining on them, he knew.

They were coming up on the road that turned into the north shore area of the lake. The same area Long supposedly had his hideout.

He was comfortably behind Lieutenant Williams now, so Mike eased off the accelerator to maintain his distance.

Mike saw another set of headlights up ahead on the right. It was John Franks blocking the only road to the north shore. Franks activated his red and blues as the chase came closer to him.

Long slowed, brake lights coming on, then he swerved toward Franks' car. Just missing the bumper, Long straightened his slide and sped up going past the turn off.

Mike saw Franks' car pull out behind him, joining the chase. Farther back, the night was illuminated by red and blue lights. The other officers were joining the chase.

The caravan was driving around eighty miles an hour again. Darkness covered the horizon. The road they were driving eventually would lead back to Colby, but it was a dangerous road.

Up ahead, brake lights flashed on from the Pathfinder. The vehicle missed a corner, swerved, over corrected, and ran into the ditch. A tire exploded from sliding on the road, and the rim threw sparks as the driver tried to accelerate.

Passing Jimmy, Mike cut in front of the Pathfinder blocking the roadway ahead. The other police cars circled the disabled Pathfinder. They came to a stop.

The Pathfinder was lit up brightly by the forward-facing takedown lights on the patrol cars' light bars. Every patrol car had them. They were all on.

Mike got out of his patrol car and took cover behind the rear of the vehicle. He was not thinking but reacting as his training took over.

Other than Jimmy and him, Franks, Amy, and Tolliver were all behind their respective cars watching the Pathfinder.

Chapter 63

Chief Tolliver watched the car go into the ditch then blow a tire as it slid back onto the pavement. He watched now with his pistol aimed in the direction of the driver side of the Pathfinder.

The driver door opened. Phil Long stepped out and ran to the front of the Pathfinder. From that point he could see all the cops, but he was hidden from a clear view. Tolliver cursed.

Phillip Long had changed a lot over the decade or more that he had been in prison. His hair was balding on top, but he had a long ponytail. He was thin to the point that his clothes hung on him. He looked around, talking to himself.

Long yelled out, "I ain't goin' back to prison."

"You got a lot to answer for. The judge will decide prison or not," Tolliver said.

"Chief? You sonofabitch! I owe you for killing my old man."

Tolliver saw the others glance at him briefly, then back to Long.

"Your dad killed himself. I had nothing to do with that."

"You liar!"

"He was a thief, stole a lot of money over time. You know that though. Your mom told you all about it. Is that why you had her attacked?"

"They were supposed to warn her from talking to you. I didn't mean to hurt her like that."

"What are we going to do now?" Tolliver asked.

"This is you and me, Chief. We meet in the street out here and settle it. Just us."

Tolliver laughed, "You watched too many bad movies in the joint, Phil. That isn't how this works. We got everyone but you."

Long looked around at the officers. He then ran back to the passenger side of the Pathfinder and got in. He switched the key on, and the driver window came down halfway.

"I got a gun. I will shoot myself if you don't get back."

"Chief?" Jimmy asked. He was squatting down at the bed of his pickup. His only weapon was the Glock in his hand.

"Everybody stay calm. Amy, call this in as a barricaded subject. See who is available."

A minute later she stood beside Tolliver, "Ranger and the DPS guy are on their way. The deputies are busy on the other side of the county."

Tolliver nodded. He wished he had a SWAT team. He looked at the others still taking cover behind their vehicles. This was the SWAT team.

Chapter 64

Ranger Murphy and DPS Sergeant Weeps pulled up parking behind Tolliver. They turned out their lights to avoid backlighting the officers.

Murphy flipped his cigarette away, exhaling a stream of smoke as he walked up to Tolliver who stood talking with Jimmy at the rear of Jimmy's pickup.

"What kind of weapon does he have?" Murphy asked.

"We haven't seen one," Jimmy said, giving an update on what had happened.

"We need to move in on him, then," Weeps said.

"Just 'cause we ain't seen a weapon, doesn't mean he ain't got one," Tolliver said.

Approaching headlights lit the group up. They all squatted down some to avoid being seen in the light by the suspect.

The car came to a stop. Jimmy recognized Janet Long's car. She came running toward the officers.

Jimmy placed his hands on her to slow her down. She was crying, and makeup running down her face left streaks of black on her cheeks.

"Please! Let me talk to my son," she said, trying to push past Jimmy.

"Janet, we don't know what he's going to do. He may have a gun," Tolliver said.

"Let me talk to him, please. I can get him to listen."

She was nearly screaming at Tolliver and pushing against Jimmy at the same time.

Phil must have seen or heard his mother's voice. He rolled the driver window all the way down and started yelling also.

"Mom! Mom! You bastards don't hurt her."

"Phillip?" Janet said.

Tolliver looked at Murphy, then at Jimmy.

"Let 'er go, Jimmy." He took Janet's arm, "I can't let you go to the vehicle, but you can talk to him from here. Where it's safe."

Janet nodded. Tolliver, with Jimmy and Amy following close behind, led Janet to his car.

Phil, from inside his car, yelled again, "You lied to me from the start. All of you are liars."

Janet broke from Tolliver's grip, causing him to stumble as she ran to Phil's car yelling. Phil got out of his car and hugged his mother.

Mother and son were holding each other for a moment, crying on the other's shoulder.

Phil broke the embrace. He shoved his mother to the ground. He then kicked her hard in the face. The impact bloodying her face as she screamed in pain.

He jerked her to her feet, "You aren't going to win this time, you bastard," he yelled toward the group of officers.

Shoving his mom against the side of the Pathfinder, he punched her in the face with his closed fist. He hit her again and again.

Chapter 65

Taken by surprise at the sudden violence against his own mother, Mike Collins ran toward the Pathfinder. He was facing the passenger side of the vehicle so he could only see the arm movements of Phil Long as he swung toward his mother.

From the corner of his eye, he saw Tolliver and the rest of the officer's rush forward at the same time.

Mike laid hands on Long first. He spun him around, breaking up the assault on his mother.

Janet fell to the ground bleeding from her face and mouth. She was on her hands and knees crying and gagging.

Long spun around out of the grasp of Mike, pushing him back hard. Long braced himself, swinging at Tolliver with a right hand that glanced off his shoulder.

Long reached into his pocket and pulled a pocket-knife. He never got to open it.

Jimmy, Murphy, Weeps and Amanda all tackled Phil Long to the ground. Franks jumped in the last moment and offered what little assistance he could in the melee.

Mike recovered enough to offer his help, though it was minimal. There were a swarm of cops on top of Long, who was trying to fight loose. Some of the cops, though he couldn't tell who, were hitting Long. Some were holding him. All were yelling at him.

Mike bent down to check on Janet Long, who was still on hands and knees where she had fallen.

She was crying, and there was a tooth on the ground mixed with the blood. She spat a lump of bloody phlegm onto the ground.

Mike radioed for EMS. He helped Janet stand. She looked at him with tears in her eyes.

"Don't hurt him, please."

Mike said nothing. From the corner of his eye, he saw Jimmy pick a handcuffed Phil Long up from the ground. The fight seemed to have gone from Phil. His clothes were dirty, and his shirt was torn. Otherwise, he looked fine.

Mike led Janet to his patrol car to await the arrival of the ambulance. He reached into his glove box where he kept paper towels and gave her some. She pressed it to her face.

Jimmy and Amy led Phil to Tolliver's patrol car, placing him in the back seat. All was quiet for the moment.

From a distance, sirens blared through the silence. EMS was on scene.

Chapter 66

Two days had passed since the chase and arrest of Phil Long. His mother had phoned the office to invite Tolliver over for a visit. He stood uncomfortably on the porch as the front door opened.

Janet Long looked as good as could be expected. The bruising to her face had started to heal and was turning various shades of purple. She invited him in.

The tooth she had lost as a result of being beaten by her son was a back molar. Tolliver couldn't tell as he noticed her smile was still intact.

"Chief! B.J. I'm glad you could make it," she said as she offered him a seat on the couch.

He sat down as she sat in an upholstered chair across from him. Janet had lived in this same house for as long as Tolliver could remember. He glanced down the hallway to the bathroom where his friend, her husband, had shot himself.

Catching his look, Janet said, "That was a long time ago."

"Seems more relevant now than it did a few months ago."

"In light of what happened, I guess so. I feel partly to blame for what Phillip done."

"He's a grown man. He made his choices. Bad as they were, he's the one to blame. The other night, he was high on his own dope. Doctors think that's why he attacked you. Not your fault."

"If I hadn't poisoned him with my own hatred of what happened all those years ago," she said.

Janet was silent a long time. The sound of a wall clock from somewhere in the house ticking away the time was the only sound.

"I'm a foolish old woman, I guess. How can I ever make up for what I put your wife through by attacking you…"?

Tolliver interrupted her, "What happened was what happened. I don't think there is a way to make up for all those years. Harsh things were said, mean things, and not just by you. I, myself, have said some things about you that should never have come from a man's mouth."

She smiled. It was a nice smile, Tolliver thought it should be used more. Maybe it could be, someday.

He said, "We can't go back to yesterday. We can only go forward from where we are. I guess we both need practice in accepting that."

"Well, from where we are now to where we will be in the future, I can only do what I can.

"Part of why I wanted to see you was to put the past behind us. My push for the past two decades was to get you out of office. Joe Rice was your most ardent supporter. Now he's gone."

"I am well aware. I have been thinking about stepping down more and more lately," Tolliver said.

"You will have my full support to stay as long as you want. And to pick your successor. It is the least I can do to try and make up for my ignorance."

They sat silent for a moment. Tolliver was not sure how to respond. Then, slowly, they began talking of old times, better times. Memories and laughter coming easy for a while. Tolliver felt at ease for the first time in a long time, his laughter feeling genuine.

About the Author

Ronnie Ashmore is the author of several short stories and novels focusing on crime fiction and westerns.

When he is not working or writing and has some spare time, he enjoys playing golf, fishing, and traveling.

You can email him at ronnieashmorebooks@gmail.com

THANK YOU
FOR READING!

If you enjoyed this book, we would appreciate your customer
review on your book seller's website or on Goodreads.

Also, we would like for you to know that you can
find more great books like this one at
www.CreativeTexts.com